MW01180926

UNJUST
TREATMENT
The True Story of Jo Ann Dewey
& The Wilson Brothers

This original work has the seal of
the copyright office in accordance
with title 17, USC and has been
made a part of the Copyright
Office of Records.
Date: May 9, 1999
TXu 901-827

A Novel Based On A True Story By:
Joan Mae Carter

DEDICATION
**This book is dedicated to anyone who has been
treated unjustly.**

CONTENTS

INTRODUCTION

This is what I know to be true: Jesus said "I tell you the truth" which means listen up, pay attention, something good is coming, and I'm going to reveal something to you. This is a mystery that spans several generations and destroys multiple lives. The ones who have survived this mystery are living with scars, both physical and mental. This revelation is called "Unjust Treatment" but not because I'm looking for justice. I think too much time has passed and I don't even know if anyone is still interested in something that took place over half a century ago. Right now my only purpose is to shed some light for anyone who wants to lift up the rocks in their lives and let the vermin scatter.

The question I had to ask myself was this, "What is gnawing at my brain that I can't put my finger on?"

You see, most people think when traumatic events happen to a person it stands to reason that you would remember the event because it was so devastating, "How could you possibly not remember it?" When in fact for a lot of people it is just the opposite, in order to survive severe trauma you have to bury it in your mind.   Each person and situation is different. Some people bury traumatic events by tossing a little dirt on it and leaving it alone, while others dig a deep hole, cover it with heavy clay, stomp the clay down and then toss on some topsoil, then to disguise the grave they plant flowers in the topsoil and go about living life smiling like nothing happened.

This story is about removing the flowers, digging up the soil and exposing darkness to the light. As a great prophet once said, "then deep from the earth you shall speak, from low in the dust your words shall come, your voice shall come from the ground like the voice of a ghost and your speech shall whisper out of the dust."

CHAPTER ONE

"THE PROPAGATOR"

A fingernail slice of the moon hung in the night sky that evening while an eight year old girl was feeling excruciating pain in her shoulders as she held her eyes closed so tightly even that was painful.

"I said open your eyes and look!" her mother commanded as she held the little girl's wrists behind her back and jerked up on her arms.

The newest jolt of pain in the Propagator's shoulders popped her eyes wide open. The child found herself in a large, unfamiliar room.

There was a crowd of about 40 people in the basement room of the Fisher Grange Hall, men, women, and children. She could see adults wearing black costumes, but it wasn't Halloween or time to go "Trick or Treating." The Propagator knew that her older sister was also in the room somewhere but she couldn't see her. Her sister was usually a source of comfort to The Propagator in situations like this, but this time there were too many people.

A door opened at the end of the room and a teenage girl dressed in a white satin gown was tied to an old wooden chair. The girl's wrists were bound to the arms of the chair with white strips of cloth. There was a matching gag in her mouth. Even though she couldn't speak, her eyes stressed the tremendous terror she felt. The girl's chair was pushed into the center of the room where people formed a circle around her.

The Propagator saw that two white enamel pans, trimmed in a black stripe around the top were placed underneath the girl's feet and she wondered to herself what they were there for.

A masked person stepped out of the circle and walked over to a tray of medical instruments beside the chair. One of the instruments on the tray was a scalpel. The black costumed person picked up the scalpel, bent down to where the girl's legs were strapped to the chair legs and sliced the young girl's femoral arteries. Blood flowed quickly out of her body and down her legs that worked as a funnel then into the two enamel pans beneath her feet. The Propagator now realized what the enamel pans were for as they filled up with blood.

As the healthy pink tint of life drained from the brown-haired girl's face, it was replaced with the bluish gray color of death. The Propagator wanted to look elsewhere but knew if she looked away her mother would inflict another jolt of pain to her arms. So she focused on a crescent shaped scar on the young girl's right cheek and she wondered about that unique mark. It was surprising that you could see anything on the young girl's face because she had been beaten severely during the abduction. The Propagator's mind wandered as she thought about the many scars on her little body. Then she heard muted struggling from the girl in the chair who was struggling in vain to stay alive. When the struggling stopped, the Propagator returned her attention to the now lifeless teenager. The girl's head had slumped toward the hardwood floor. The white satin dress now had a red hem of blood around the bottom.

The Propagator had to watch as people descended like vultures on a spent carcass. They removed the ceremonial gown, and proceeded to defile the girl's sacrificed body. They took the scalpel and cut the light brown circles of her breast from her body, then ripped the tops of her breasts off. They took the same bloody scalpel and carved an upside down "U" shape around her pubic mound and flopped her pubic skin down over her rectum. She could also see that the girl's rectum had been mutilated even before the cutting began.

A few days later it was time for the Propagator to go for a car ride with her father. She knew it wasn't a family outing because her mother and sister were staying home. Like an exuberant puppy, she scrambled for the backseat. She didn't know why she always wanted to sit in the back seat when her father wanted to go for a drive, maybe some day she'd figure it out.

"Oh no you don't, come on get in the front seat," he said as he grabbed his daughter by the shoulder. He pressed his fingers into her clavicle so hard she wriggled away from his painful touch. Physical contact with her father was always painful.

It was a short drive through the little town of Washougal, Washington out to the main highway that led east up the beautiful Columbia Gorge. The road was windy and narrow and there were few cars. Once in a while a car would get in front of the big old black sedan and her father couldn't stand it. Even at the shortest straight stretches in the road he would edge the car to the left far enough to catch a peek to see if there was any oncoming traffic. Then he would pull into the lane of oncoming traffic, gun it and leave the slower moving vehicle far behind as he merged back to the right side of the road.

Inside the car, the Propagator would sit as close as she could to the passenger door, she'd only have half her body on the seat. She always tried her best to stay out of her father's reach.

She was a curious youngster and she'd peek out the car window to see the different kinds of cars they were passing on the road. After awhile there were no more cars to peek at.

As they passed through the town of Carson, Washington, she could hear the sound of crunching gravel beneath the tires and wondered what happened to the smooth road. Her father stopped the car.

"Get out," he commanded.

She hopped out of the car immediately, but was startled to see how close her father had parked to the edge of a steep canyon. She stood there frozen as he came around the front of the car. That "look" had materialized in his eyes again. There was nowhere to run and nowhere to hide. Her little body sank into submission. He picked up his daughter and walked out into the middle of the old suspension bridge that hung 260 feet above the Wind River. He lifted his daughter by her armpits up and over the side of the bridge and held her over a deep ravine. The swift, raging waters below foamed like a rabid mouth as if the water would eat her alive. She dangled there like a rag doll while he shook and yelled at her.

"Don't you ever tell anyone what you saw, do you hear me?"

She nodded her head as her father shook her some more.

"And don't you even think about talking to those men with the badges, you got that?"

She was crying now as she nodded her head again.

"I can't hear the shit rolling around in your brain, answer me girl."

"Yes."

"Yes, what?"

"I promise not to tell," she managed to choke out in between terrified sobs.

"If you ever tell anyone, we'll do the same thing to you," he threatened as he kicked a loose stone from the bridge over the edge and down into the canyon. She watched the rock ping pong it's way down the steep crevasse until it was swallowed up by the rapidly moving Wind River.

Her father retracted his arms and lugged his daughter back to the car where he threw the Propagator to the ground beside the big black tires on the car. She scrambled to her feet. Her tear stained face was waiting for the next command from her father and the next wave of humiliating pain that was as sure to come, as sure as the sun falling down behind the Evergreen-lined walls of the Wind River Canyon.

"Now get back in the car," he ordered as he pulled out an unfiltered Camel cigarette from his rolled up shirtsleeve and lit it up.

CHAPTER TWO

"THE ABDUCTION"

It was a little after 11:00 PM on Sunday, March 19, 1950 when Jo Ann Dewey arrived in downtown Vancouver, Washington while the last quarter of the moon hung like a slice of a fingernail in the dark sky that warm spring evening. She had spent the day working in the kitchen at the Portland Sanitarium until 7:00 PM. Her friend Joan Crawford met her after work and they went to the Paramount Theater together. They saw the show, "Samson and Delilah". When it was over, Joan took Jo Ann to the Portland bus depot. Joan bought Jo Ann a one way ticket to Vancouver.

It was a short ride from Portland across the big Interstate Bridge that connected Washington State and Oregon State. Although she was tired after a hard day's work of cleaning and dishwashing she didn't have time to doze off on the short bus ride.

The Vancouver bus depot was familiar to Jo Ann as she had made the trip from Portland, Oregon to Vancouver, Washington after work many times. She used the public payphone in the depot to call her mother who worked at a nursing home in Battle Ground, about 70 miles Northeast of Vancouver.

"Hi mom it's me, how's work going?"

"It's really busy tonight, where are you?" her mother asked.

"I'm at the Vancouver bus depot, I was calling to find a way home."

"Jo Ann, I can't get any ride for you 'cause you know we don't have a phone at the house. I think you're going to have to go over to St. Joseph's hospital."

"Is Mrs. Crull there?"

"Yes, she's working the graveyard shift, stay with her until her shift is over and then ride home with her and I'll pick you up at her house first thing in the morning."

"Okay, I'll head over there right now, see you tomorrow Mother."

"Okay, I love you."

"Love you too, bye."

Trusting that her daughter was taken care of and that she would see her daughter in the morning when their neighbor Dora Crull brought Jo Ann home with her, Mrs. Dewey returned to her evening duties at the Meadow Glade Nursing Home.

Jo Ann slipped her purse over her shoulder, thankful that her older brother had fixed the broken strap. Then she adjusted the two gold barrettes in her hair before stepping outside. It was unseasonably warm and dry for that particular time of year in the northwest, but Jo Ann buttoned up all the buttons on her heavy coat out of habit as she headed out of the bus depot into the dimly lit empty streets of Vancouver. She was obeying her mother's instructions to walk the short distance to St. Joseph's hospital and to wait for her neighbor to get off work so she could get a ride home.

She hadn't gotten far when a dark sedan with two men in it pulled up beside her. She pretended not to notice the car as a chill ran down her spine despite the warmth of her overcoat.

"Get in the car," a man's voice demanded forcefully from the open window.

"No!" She exclaimed and took off running down the sidewalk.

The driver kept the car running as he slammed on the brakes and shoved the gear shift into park. He quickly turned off the headlights as another man jumped out the passenger door. The passenger was tall and had a Frankenstein-shaped head. He also had long legs that allowed him to easily catch up and over take Jo Ann. He grabbed her by the back collar of her coat and as she was jerked backwards the top button popped off her coat. She immediately started screaming for help as she struggled to get out of the man's grasp. During the struggle she slipped out of her coat and took off running again. She managed only to get about twenty feet away from the car when the assailant overtook her again. This time he tackled her to the ground and started to pummel her about the head. He inflicted severe blows to the chin causing Jo Ann to become dizzy. She stopped screaming when she felt teeth fall from her mouth.

When he felt the disheveled body start to lose it's will to put up a struggle, he helped her up on her feet. He put one arm around her shoulder and acted like he was escorting a companion to the idling car parked on the side of the road. As her head cleared, she regained some of her senses and began to scream and struggle against the staged charade. It was at this point the driver of the car knew he had to get more involved. He was a short, small-boned man, with dark, slicked-back hair. He liked to stay lurking in the shadows while others did his dirty work but this time it looked like he was going to have to get dirt under his fingernails. He got out of the car and opened the back passenger side door so Jo Ann could be stuffed into the back seat. From months of lifting heavy plates and bowls in the kitchen at the Portland Sanitarium, she was very muscular for her young age. It was hard for the two grown men to handle her. On top of that, adrenalin pumped through her body and she knew she needed to put up the fight of her life.

Summoned by the blood-curdling screams from Jo Ann a gallery of residents from a nearby apartment complex had assembled outside to see what was going on.

"Hey, what's up?" one of the residents shouted.

"Shut up, it's my wife," the tall man responded.

"No I'm not! No I'm not!" Jo Ann screamed as loud as she could while at the same time her two kidnappers were still struggling to get her stuffed into the back seat of the black sedan.

A quick boxer's punch to her chin subdued Jo Ann enough to be placed in the car. Then the taller of the two abductors quickly picked up the coat Jo Ann had wriggled out of and slung it over his arm. He tossed the coat onto the front seat beside him, put the car in gear and took off like a rocket. The "car of death" had been swallowed up in the dark.

The high powered car was in good running condition as it cruised at high speed down the Camas-Orchard Highway to 164th Avenue and pulled into the gravel parking lot of the Fisher's Grange Hall in less than ten minutes. The Pomona Grand Master of the grange hall had the doors of the building unlocked and the building prepared to receive the victim.

In Vancouver, Washington the police station is six blocks away from 12th and D Streets. It would take policemen less than two minutes to arrive there by car. On Sunday night, March 19, 1950 the call came into the Vancouver Police Station. The dispatcher was informed by an eyewitness that someone was assaulting a woman.

"Edmonds," the dispatcher called, "some guy's beating up his wife in front of the Central Court Apartments and took off with her, can you roll on that?"

"I'm on my way," responded the officer as he headed out the door of the police station and stepped into the patrol car being driven by his partner.

Officer Estel Perry and Officer Harold Edmonds were the first two policemen at the scene of the crime.

Carl Adolph Forsbeck, a sergeant who doesn't usually go out on calls, heard the dispatcher and headed out the door too. Just then a rookie by the name of Frank Irvin was heading into the station to pick up his usual partner. Forsbeck summoned him to go with him in a second car, to the scene.

"Let me out here," said Forsbeck to Irvin as their police car sped it's way down the narrow city streets, lined with parked cars.

"Why here?" the rookie asked, "the apartment building is still another block away."

"I need to look around for tire tracks," said Forsbeck.

Irvin thought it was odd to look for tire tracks on the paved roads, but he obeyed his superior officer. He stopped the car and Forsbeck got out.

"Now you go on down the street, and be on the look out for any suspicious vehicles."

"Yes sir," said the rookie.

Irvin drove to where Officer's Perry and Edmonds were taking statements from the apartment building residents.

After listening to their statements and taking notes, Irvin saw Forsbeck walking towards him.

"Did you find any tire tracks?" asked Officer Irvin.

"None, but I bet if we go back to the scene of the crime we might find some evidence, let's drive back there."

Officer Irvin and Sergeant Forsbeck got back in the patrol car and headed to 13th and D Streets.

"Shine the headlights in the middle of the road, I think I see something," said Forsbeck.

"Hand me my flashlight," said Irvin as he stopped the car.

Forsbeck handed him the flashlight and got out of the car. They looked around and quickly found a black plastic purse strap and a gold colored barrette along with a beer bottle in the middle of the road, garbage or evidence?

CHAPTER THREE

"MISSING"

Still wearing her nurse's nightcap and black dress with white-lace collar, Jo Ann's mother, Anna Dewey knocked on the door of her friend and neighbor, Dora Crull. When Dora came to the door Anna told her she was there to pick up her daughter.

"Jo Ann isn't here," said Dora, perplexed.

"What do you mean she isn't here? She was supposed to walk over to St. Joe's and come home with you after your shift last night," explained Anna.

"I had no idea, what time was that?"

"Oh, let's see, I was really busy around eleven last night, I think that's when she called."

"Oh gracious mercy," said Dora in alarm, "you say it was around eleven o'clock?"

"Yes why?"

"Oh no, I better go see if Jo Ann's been in her room," she exclaimed as she turned and ran towards her own home as fast as her plump, 40 year old body would carry her.

Anna Dewey arrived at the Vancouver police station and walked into the front office where a uniformed policeman was sitting behind a desk. Mrs. Dewey inquired about filing a missing person's report.

"What seems to be the problem?" the officer asked.

"I can't find my…" started Mrs. Dewey when the officer interrupted her.

"First things first ma'am, what's your name?" asked the officer as he rummaged through miscellaneous police-type paraphernalia at the front desk until he found a Missing Persons Information sheet attached to a clipboard and a pen.

As the rummaging subsided, she answered his first question, "Mrs. Clyde Dewey."

"Address?"

"Route two, Box 258, Battle Ground," she continued.

"Telephone number?"

"We don't have a telephone."

"And, who is it that you think might be missing?"

"My daughter."

"What's her name?"

"Jo Ann Dewey"

"How old is she?"

"She just turned 18."

"How long has she been missing?"

"Well, I went to pick her up this morning at our neighbor's house, just as soon as I got off the nightshift, but Mrs. Crull says she never saw her."

"Does your daughter live with you?"

"No, she lives with friends in Portland by the Sanitarium where she works, but she comes home on weekends so we keep a bedroom for her at the house."

"Okay, what does your daughter look like, let's start with how tall is she?"

"She's about 5' 4."

"Weight?"

"About 160 pounds."

"Hair color?"

"She has short, brown, curly hair."

"Does she have any unusual features or identifying birthmarks?"

"Yes, she has a crescent shaped scar on her right cheek."

"Do you know what she was wearing last?"

"Well, I'm pretty sure she was wearing her regular coat."

"Describe the coat please."

"It's brown, and long, it hangs just below her knees."

"Okay, what else was she wearing?"

"She sometimes wears her uniform home so I assume she would have had on a blue skirt and white blouse with white bobby sox and I know she carries a black purse cause I know my son fixed the broken handle on it for her just last week."

"Can you wait here a minute, I'm going to go get my supervisor, I'll be right back."

The alarm Mrs. Dewey felt earlier after talking to her neighbor about the screams intensified immensely as she waited for the officer to return with his supervisor.

"Mrs. Dewey, this officer would like you to follow him to his office just down the hallway."

"Do you know where my daughter is?" Mrs. Dewey inquired.

"Mrs. Dewey would you please follow me to my office?"

"Where's my daughter?"

"Come this way please, I'd like you to take a look at something."

It felt like her shoes were lined with lead as she walked behind the police officer but she didn't know why. She also felt like she didn't want to be there, yet needing answers about her "baby-girl" she forced her feet to shuffle in a forward motion.

"Have a seat please," the officer said as he motioned towards a single chair situated on one side of his desk and then he closed the door to his office.

After she was seated, the officer sat down in his chair behind the big wooden desk across from her.

"I'd like you to take a look at a couple of items I have," he said as he reached into his desk drawer and pulled out a gold barrette and a black, plastic purse strap.

Like a sucker punch to the stomach a wave of nauseous panic gripped and froze the gentle woman. She felt like running away from the items on the desk. As if she could somehow distance herself from the barrette and purse strap then it wouldn't be true that those items belonged to her missing daughter.

CHAPTER FOUR

"THE VICTIM"

Jo Ann Dewey was born on October 16, 1931 in Lone Pine, Montana. She was the youngest daughter of Noble Clyde and Anna Eunice Dewey. Her older siblings included four brothers, James, Burton, Clyde and Ivan Dale. Jo Ann also had two older sisters, Lyla and Grace. She was a girl who made friends easily and had a lot of them.

After High School, Jo Ann attended the Columbia Academy in Vancouver. At the time of her disappearance she was washing dishes at the Portland Sanitarium in Portland, Oregon.

On Friday, March 24, 1950, five days after Jo Ann's mother reported her missing, Mayor Vern Anderson of Vancouver, called a conference of the local law enforcement heads. The conference included Vancouver Police Chief Harry Diamond and Sheriff Earl Anderson also of Vancouver. At that time Sheriff Anderson was appointed by the mayor to head the entire investigation. The sheriff made plans to launch an all out search over the weekend.

Early Saturday morning a mass of citizen volunteers gathered outside Vancouver City Hall with cars and trucks. Concerned citizens showed up in old clothes and were taken aside on the courthouse lawn for instructions. Approximately 500 people had shown up. It was the largest outpouring of volunteers Clark County, Washington had ever seen. From the Pacific Highway in Hazel Dell down to the Columbia River where a new mausoleum was being constructed, an extensive search was made but nothing was found.

It wouldn't be until Sunday March 26, 1950, a full week after Jo Ann's disappearance, when three fishermen embarked on a journey, that would bring the search to an end.

Starting out from their hometown of Yakima, Washington, Gerry Frandle and Bob Rummel headed north up old Highway 97. It was still dark out at 4:30 in the morning when the duo left the dew-sparkled rolling brown hills of the Yakima valley. It was a 17 mile drive up small inclines and around sharp corners to get to Tieton, Washington where their other fishing buddy Ray Lowry lived.

Within twenty minutes the eager fishing duo was pulling into Ray's driveway. After hastily stowing Ray's gear in the trunk the threesome hit the road. Gerry drove a steady 55 MPH all the way to Highway 14 near Lyle. Gerry knew the exact fishing spot he wanted to take his buddies to. After passing through the small town of Lyle they ended up in an even smaller town called Carson, where eventually the paved roads turned into gravel roads with large potholes. After swerving and dodging potholes for what seemed like an eternity, Gerry pulled the car off to the side of the road and parked next to a forest of old growth Washington State evergreen trees.

"We're here guys."

"Ah, good ole Wind River, I hear the fish just waiting to jump on my hook," said Bob.

"Swell, let's go," said Ray as he pulled up on the door handle and got out of the car.

Bob was next to get out of the car. He put his hands on his hips, arched his back and looked up towards the gray sky. Small droplets of rain hit his face and made him blink. It was about 8:30 in the morning when Gerry opened the trunk of the car so they could get out their gear. It didn't take long for all three of them to don their favorite fishing garb. They each had their reels on their poles and the poles balanced on their shoulders as they headed into the woods.

The long poles bobbed up and down rhythmically as the men walked down the deer-made trail path. Single-file they walked a pole's length apart from each other. With each step the sound of the swiftly flowing Wind River became louder. When the woods parted like curtains on an opening night performance and one by one the fishermen broke through the darkness of the forest, each of them smiled as they laid their eyes on the Holy Grail of fishing spots.

"Hey do you guys smell something?" asked Gerry as he slid down a half-frozen dirt embankment.

"Yea, something stinks," agreed Ray as he followed Gerry down the dirt and onto the rocky riverbank.

"Smells like someone poached a deer and left it," chimed in Bob as he followed suit.

"Wait a minute, I think I see something out there in the middle of the river."

"It's just the sand bar."

"No it's not, I see something too, maybe it's a poached deer."

"No, it doesn't look like an animal."

"It looks pretty big, let's go check it out."

"Hey, have you guys been following the story of that missing girl? Maybe it's her."

"Can't be."

"Hey, it could be, come on let's wade over there and see."

Ray, Gerry and Bob with their hip-waders on stepped into the swift moving, icy-cold water of the Wind River. As they approached the gravel bar the object of their curiosity became clear. It was a body. It was lying face down in about six inches of shallow water. The gravel bar had snagged the body and kept it from floating any farther down stream.

"Wow!" Ray exclaimed pointing the end of his fishing pole over the bloated lifeless form.

"Hey, don't touch it man!" Gerry yelled.

"I wasn't," said Ray.

"Do you think it's a girl's body? You know the one that was kidnapped? The one from Vancouver?"

"You mean the one that's been in the news?"

"Yep, that one."

"I don't know but if it is we better get to a phone and call the police," said Bob.

"I think there's a hotel just about a quarter mile or so up that trail," said Gerry as he pointed towards the left bank of the river.

The three fishermen hurried through the rain up the trail to the St. Martin's Hot Springs Hotel. Once there, the hotel manager immediately telephoned the proper authorities.

Sheriff Earl Anderson, the lead investigator appointed by the mayor of Vancouver and a deputy from Clark County arrived first. They were followed by detectives, the Coroner, more officers and news reporters. It was almost noon, but it was still cold and dreary out so someone decided to build a small fire on the riverbank. About a dozen people huddled around the orange flames discussing the discovery.

Sheriff Anderson and his deputy borrowed the fishermen's hip boots and waded out to the body. Even through the thick rubber of the waders they could feel the cold water swiftly rushing past their legs.

Sheriff Anderson had the police department's camera with him and took the first pictures of the body without touching it. Then he turned the naked body over to expose a mutilated form that was definitely female.

"It looks like we may have found the Dewey girl!" called Sheriff Anderson to the Coroner who was waiting at the water's edge with a stretcher and a blanket.

"I'm sending out some more guys to help you two bring her in," hollered the Coroner through cupped hands around his mouth.

Four volunteers waded out to the gravel bar in the middle of the river to help the sheriff and his deputy carry the bloated body to shore.

At the shore the bloated body was wrapped in a blanket and taken away. Some news reporters followed the Coroner's Ambulance while other reporters stayed at the crime scene and interviewed the three fishermen who discovered the body.

Sheriff Anderson conducted an immediate search for any kind of evidence. He instructed detectives, the police and volunteer searchers to search the wild wooded area in eastern Skamania County and a labyrinth of secluded hiking trails. There were empty hunters cabins in the area and they were searched extensively. Sheriff Anderson and his deputy searched the suspension bridges as well as a nearby garbage dump but not a single stitch of evidence such as clothing turned up anywhere.

Present at the body dump location was Oregon State Patrolman, Harold Cusic, a close friend of the Dewey family. He made positive identification that the body found in the Wind River near the city of Carson, was in fact Jo Ann Dewey.

Police Chief Harry Diamond drove out to the Dewey home in Meadow Glade to perform the grim task of telling the family about Jo Ann's body being found. Meanwhile her mother had been maintaining a ceaseless vigil at her home, praying continuously and hoping that the next person to walk through the front door of her home would be her youngest child. That would never happen.

Sheriff Anderson was in charge of Jo Ann's dead body. He decided to have it taken to Dr. Howard Richardson, a Vancouver pathologist who performed autopsies. Sheriff Anderson remained present during the entire autopsy and helped take more pictures. After the autopsy, Jo Ann's body was taken to the Evergreen Funeral Home to be prepared for a closed casket funeral and burial.

Exactly ten days after her blood curdling, screams echoed through that late Sunday night in March, Jo Ann's body was laid to rest. Over 800 people flocked to the small, Seventh Day Adventist Church in Meadow Glade which is approximately one mile southwest of Battle Ground. Among the assemblage were Jo Ann's parents and her six older siblings.

"We are gathered here together to pay our last respects to a young girl whose life was taken away before her natural demise," recited Pastor McKeown, as the Meadow Glade Male Quartet hummed soft dirges in the background. "No one can know what might have been if she had not been taken on that fatal night. As you can all clearly see by the crowd here today Jo Ann befriended many people. Through the shocking news reports, the county, the city and our entire nation has been made aware of this unjustified death of an innocent girl."

The funeral went on for an hour. Finally the last note from the organ resonated into silence at the church.

Ben Ward, Calvin Rowart, Joe Cusic, Don Schaffer, Tom Gray and Dale Walker, all close friends of the Dewey family, served as Pallbearers. They lifted the basic casket onto their shoulders with the lifeless child inside. Eight of Jo Ann's friends were Honorary Pallbearers and lined up behind the casket four to a side.

Schoolmates of Jo Ann's from the Columbia Academy carried sixty-five floral wreaths. The ambiance in the church was that of an English Tea Garden.

The coffin was slid into the back of the hearse, the double doors were closed and the driver was given the okay signal to drive away. Once again Jo Ann Dewey was being moved in a dark vehicle against her will. This time however, the transportation vehicle was slow moving and she had hundreds of loving people behind her in their cars. The single file procession of cars received a police escort from the Meadow Glade Church to the Brush Prairie Cemetery. The cavalcade of cars stretched out for miles along the road.

The Brush Prairie Cemetery was in the middle of nowhere with nothing around for miles. The entire graveyard was void of trees and foliage. Only a patch of neatly mowed lawn around grave markers was the evidence that people were resting in peace there. Jo Ann's final resting place was selected to be in the center of the cemetery. An expensive headstone was purchased through donations from friends. Carved into the marble were two flowers in the upper corners and an oval picture of Jo Ann's beautiful, smiling face was inlaid in the middle. The inscription in all capital letters read; "IN LOVING MEMORY OF JO ANN DEWEY, 1931-1950 FROM HER FRIENDS."

The graveside service was very short, final rites from the twenty third Psalm was read out of the King James Bible.

> *"The Lord is my shepherd; I shall not want. He maketh me to lie down in green pastures; He leadeth me beside the still waters. He restoreth my soul; He leadeth me in the paths of righteousness for His name's sake. Yea, though I walk through the valley of the shadow of death, I will fear no evil; for Thou art with me; Thy rod and Thy staff they comfort me. Thou preparest a table before me in the presence of mine enemies; Thou anointest my head with oil; my cup runneth over. Surely goodness and mercy shall follow me all the days of my life; and I will dwell in the house of the Lord forever."*

CHAPTER FIVE

"THE WILSON BROTHERS"

In the 1940's, World War II was in full swing and Edward R. Murrow won acclaim as a news commentator with his on-the-scene radio reporting. In the sports world Joe DiMaggio led the New York Yankees to the World Series and a Norwegian figure skater named Sonja Henie, won three Olympic gold medals. The most popular actor in Hollywood was Clark Gable who was cast as Rhett Butler in "Gone with the Wind." At fifteen, child star Shirley Temple was considered over the hill and making unsuccessful films. She would soon retire; while at the same time a totally unknown fifteen-year-old would soon rise to notorious infamy, his name was Turman Gallile Wilson.

Turman was born on March 28, 1926 in Arkansas. He was the fourth son of Mose and Eunice Wilson. After spending some time in Kansas where Turman's younger brother Utah Wilson was born their father uprooted the family to the State of Washington. They were labeled "Dust Bowl Migrants". Turman attended Shumway Junior High School in Vancouver but quit in the eighth grade at the age of fifteen. He was described as being a nuisance to the women teachers but with men instructors he showed a little more respect as long as discipline was strict and rigidly enforced. It was reported as common knowledge among the teachers that Turman had to be watched at all times because he was "tricky."

Turman and Utah Wilson were certainly not innocent of criminal behavior. It was recorded by the warden of the Oregon State Penitentiary in Salem that the Wilson Family had a long criminal record. So to sugar coat or paint a rosy picture of the boy's past would hot be accurate.

At sixteen Turman got in trouble with his two older brothers, Glenn and Rassi Wilson. They raped two 17-year old girls in Portland, Oregon. Turman plead guilty to rape and was sentenced to the Oregon State Penitentiary for seven years. His older brother Glenn got ten years and Rassi Wilson got over twenty. Shortly after his incarceration he escaped from the penitentiary and stole an automobile. After being recaptured he received an additional sentence of 18 months.

In all, Turman was in the Oregon State Penitentiary on two felony convictions from the age of sixteen until he was twenty-two. After he settled down and did his time he was released early for good behavior on April 16, 1948. He had been incarcerated for more than six years of his young life. After his release from prison he returned to Camas, Washington to live with his divorced mother Eunice Wilson. A few months after moving back home he held up a service station in Portland where he stole thirty five dollars. He was arrested on a misdemeanor and jail time was added to his criminal record.

After this Turman worked picking berries and doing general farm work. Then in October of 1949 he got the break he was hoping would turn his life around. A steady job that he hoped would give him some dignity and self respect. He got a job working at the Washougal Woolen Mills. He started off as a "Tacker" then he became a "Washer's Helper" where he washed and shrunk material. At the age of 24 he was making $1.20 an hour. He stood 5' 7" tall and weighed around 150 pounds. He had dark brown hair and thick eyebrows that sat in between a high forehead and dark brown solemn eyes. Even though he had a fairly broad nose this balanced out his full lips and perfectly rounded chin.

Turman's younger brother Utah was born on January 29, 1930 in the Sunflower State of Kansas. He was the youngest of six brothers. He got labeled a "poor student" and "a troublemaker" by the Vancouver school staff. With no motivation to continue his studies he became an illiterate, ninth grade drop out.

Utah's criminal history began getting recorded in the town of Chehalis, Washington at a juvenile detention center also known as a "training school" for boys. Today the old training school is still being used as a boy's detention center and sits alongside the busy I-5 freeway. It's a brick building with a high chain link fence that's topped with looped barbed wire, but back in the late 1940's when Utah was sent there the school was in the middle of a hayfield.

During his detention period Utah engineered a daring escape from the training school but his freedom was short lived. He was found and returned to Chehalis. Utah settled down, finished his sentence and was released.

After his release on November 1, 1948 at the age of 18, he was arrested in Washington State on a traffic offense. During this time he decided to confess and make a clean start of his life. He admitted to committing over a dozen burglaries in a time span of a couple of months in and around Vancouver, Washington which included the Edwin Rose Grocery Store and the Glenwood Service Station.

Upon entering a plea of guilty with regards to the traffic violation Utah's sentence was deferred for two years and he was ordered to remain in jail for one year. His conduct in jail was reported as "excellent" and he was released three months early for good behavior. After his release, he got a job cutting and bucking timber on Larch Mountain which is located east of small town called Washougal, Washington. He was trained on how to use a 35 pound, gas-powered chainsaw at the age of 19. Utah was 5' 8" and weighed a slim 134 pounds but he handled the heavy commercial chainsaw well. He had brown, unkempt short hair and a round face with small ears and a slender nose which gave him impish good looks which made a spunky, petite 17 year old girl named Lucille

Atilla Cline fall in love with him. The two youngsters made a cute couple. Lucille and Utah agreed to marry in a civil ceremony on December 4, 1949. They never had a formal honeymoon and shortly after their marriage they moved into her mother's apartment in Vancouver, three blocks away from the Saint Joseph Hospital.

CHAPTER SIX

"THE ALIBI"

It was Saturday afternoon March 18, 1950, Turman and Utah were at a local dental clinic in Vancouver, Washington while a friend of theirs by the name of Carl Whitney was being detained downtown at the Vancouver Police Department. Carl was on a routine visit to his parole officer when two Vancouver detectives escorted Carl into an interrogation room. The two detectives suspected Utah of stealing the power saw from when he worked cutting and bucking timber on Larch Mountain. After a short intimidating conversation with the two detectives Carl immediately wanted to go and warn his friend about the missing power saw.

Carl was a good friend of both Mrs. and Mr. Utah Wilson ever since the three of them had met at a dance two years earlier. Whether or not the story from the Vancouver detectives was true or not, knowing that Utah was on parole Carl had a high level of concern for his friend possibly violating his parole and wanted to warn him about the missing power saw as soon as possible. So Carl headed out to his friend's apartment. Unfortunately Utah was at the dental clinic with his brother at the time so Carl passed on the information to Utah's wife, Lucille and her mother.

After Turman had his molars pulled, Utah drove his brother to their mother's house. While Turman retired early that night on pain killers and with a mouth full of cotton balls, Utah stayed and visited with his family before heading home to the apartment he shared with his young bride and mother-in-law.

The next morning was Sunday, March 19, 1950. Utah had breakfast with Lucille who related the story about the missing power saw that Carl had told them the night before. Not sure what to do, Utah drove into Camas to see his brother. He wanted to give Turman the skinny on the stolen power saw.

"Where's ma?" asked Utah, as he walked into his mother's home and found Turman still sleeping on the couch.

"She just left," Turman mumbled through swollen gums and cheeks packed with cotton.

"Turm, I'm scared."

"Why, what's going on?" asked his brother as he sat up and pulled the cotton out of his mouth then reached for a cigarette and lighter off of the coffee table in front of him.

"They can't revoke my parole I had nothing to do with that darn ole saw! I never took nothin' this time. I'm trying to get my life back on track, I don't want to mess things up now. I don't want to go back to prison, they can't pin this on me! They been trying to find somethin' to nail me with and this ain't going to be it! I left that saw where it belongs!", ranted Utah, "Lucille got a visit from our friend Carl, you remember Carl Whitney don't you?"

"Yea," said Turman calmly as he drew another breath of smoke into his lungs.

"Well, he told Lucille he heard from those damn Vancouver Detectives that a power saw had come up missing at Larch Mountain and they's thinking I had something to do with it. Carl came over to warn me while we were at the dentist's. What should we do Turm? You think they'll revoke my parole?"

"I can't say for sure, they might, those detectives and the Vancouver police hate my guts so much they'd just as soon shoot me as look at me."

"Where should we go?"

"Let's go talk to dad."

Given their father's criminal history and personal bouts with the law, Turman felt like their estranged parent would be the best advisor for their situation. So the two boys packed some clothes, toiletries and a few other belongings which included a large sum of money and a handgun, into a couple of paper grocery sacks and headed south to Oregon.

Mose Wilson lived in Silverton, Oregon a small town near Salem, the state's capital. He rented some property from a family by the name of Goodman where he parked his travel trailer. To say Mose provided a very unstable home for his family was a sugar coating. In the 1930's he was sent to the penitentiary on the charge of incest with his daughter. His other recorded crimes included assault, driving drunk and disorderly conduct.

When the boys arrived at the trailer Mose wasn't home so the boys drove around looking for him. Around four o'clock that warm Sunday afternoon in March, they found him intoxicated and staggering down the street. Turman pulled up in his car alongside his father and when Mose recognized his son he got in the car. The three of them spent the next several hours driving around. As their father sobered, they told him about Utah's situation. Mose tried to give his two frightened sons some fatherly advice but was no help at all. So the boys dropped their father off at his trailer and headed back towards home. They got on Highway 99 and drove North. Around eight o'clock on the unusually warm evening of March 19, 1950, they stopped for supper in Portland, Oregon at the Jolly Joan Restaurant.

"I think I'll just have some soup, Utah, my mouth is still really sore from going to the dentist yesterday," said Turman as he pushed open the door of the restaurant.

"Hey, how 'bout we go to the picture show after we're done eating?" Utah asked.

"Sure, we haven't been to the Playhouse Theatre in awhile lets go there," recommended Turman.

"Sounds swell," said Utah.

After eating their meal, tipping the waitress and paying the check the boys were excited to head off to the theatre. Going to the movies was one of their favorite pass times. It provided a modest escape from their otherwise troubled lives.

The old Playhouse Theatre on the corner of 11th and Morrison Streets in Portland, Oregon was not considered a first run theatre but it did a good business considering its location. Approximately one hundred people a day came to see the old movies. However, the management thought they could do better than that, so they started promoting double features of like movies and on special occasions even had the usherettes dressing in costumes to keep with the chosen theme.

There were two "Captain" movies playing on the night of March 19, 1950. The first was "Captain Caution". The movie was over a decade old and starred Victor Mature and Alan Ladd. The movie ran one hour and 25 minutes.

The second feature presented at the Playhouse Theatre that evening was another movie chosen because of the word "Captain" in its title. It was "Captain Fury". This movie was made in 1939 and ran one hour and 31 minutes. It starred June Lang and John Carradine in an adventure set in an Australian penal colony.

The promotional aspect of two "Captain" movies playing as a double feature was lost on both Turman and Utah. They didn't really care what was playing, next to sports going to the movies was one of their most favorite things to do.

After giving the outside box office usherette 85 cents a piece to get in, Turman noticed a small, blonde-haired girl, dressed in bright-red slacks and a yellow blouse, standing in the lobby. Her name was Betty Mae Lyon. She stood just a little over five feet tall even in high heels. She had shoulder length, wavy hair and a nice smile. She seemed like a very approachable person who would be easy to talk to. So Turman approached her as she stood in her brightly colored "Pirate Costume" at the curtained entrance to the theatre proper and he struck up a conversation with her.

"Hi, what's your name?"

"Betty."

"Are you new here?" Turman asked.

"Yep this is my first night," Betty replied.

"I guess you wouldn't know a girl by the name of Ingstrom that works here then would you?"

But before Betty could answer his question, a comely brunette who was listening in on the conversation from behind the refreshment bar, leaned over the counter and said, "I know that usherette."

Turman turned around and approached the older woman who was standing behind the candy counter and said, "I used to talk to her when we would come here, but since I've got a steady job at the woolen mill it's been quite awhile since my brother and I have been in here, anyway I think Ingstrom was her last name and she was the head usherette, do you know her?"

"Yes, but she no longer works here, I'm head usherette now."

"Oh I see, so what's your name?"

"Cleo Wilson."

"I'm Turman Wilson, what a coincidence we have the same last name."

"Wilson is my married name."

"Nice to meet you Mrs. Wilson"

"Nice to meet you too," Cleo replied, "would you like to buy some refreshments before the show starts?"

"Sure, I'll have an ice cream slice and I know my brother will have his usual cashew nuts, and we'll take a couple of Cokes."

"I can get you the nuts and ice cream but you'll have to get your drinks out of the Coke machine."

"Hey Utah go find the Coke machine," said Turman as he reached into his pocket and handed his brother some change.

"That'll be two bits," said Cleo as she handed Turman his ice cream and the bag of nuts.

"Eighty five cents for tickets to get in and two bits for snacks, things sure ain't cheap anymore," commented Turman as he handed the refreshment counter girl the change.

After he paid for their snacks, Utah went into the men's washroom while his brother waited for him. Then they entered the theatre proper in the dark. Betty Lyon, the Pirate Usherette for the evening escorted them down the aisle with her flashlight. The boys found two empty seats together beside a couple who looked like they could have been married which made Utah think of his Lucille back at home.

The brothers enjoyed both the old "Captain" movies. It was around midnight when the movies got over. Walking out of the musty old theatre into the unseasonably warm March air that Sunday night Utah lit up his last cigarette.

"What'd you think of that new blonde working tonight?" asked Turman.

"Well, she was prettier than that Ingstrom girl, but not as pretty as my Lucille."

"Speaking of Lucille, you two have never really had a honeymoon have you?"

"No why?"

"Well we should fix you two up with a nice honeymoon here in Portland this week, how's that sound?"

"That sounds keen," Utah said with enthusiasm as he smoked his last cigarette to the butt, then flicked it to the cement sidewalk and ground out the orange ember with his shoe.

"You need more cigs?"

"That was my last one."

"Alright, we can stop at Tony's Market and pick you up more smokes there let's get in the car and get across the bridge, I'm getting a little tired."

Turman's 10 year old, black Buick was parked on the side of the street two blocks from the Playhouse Theatre. Utah noticed the parking meter's time had expired.

"This looks like our lucky night, look Turm, no parking ticket," said Utah.

"Yeah, now let's hope she starts."

The Buick started alright but it spit and sputtered as Turman turned on the headlights, put the car in gear and chugged out onto the moonlit streets of

Portland, Oregon to start the short drive across the interstate bridge back to Washington.

It was after midnight when Turman knocked on the glass door of "Tony's Day'N Nite" market. The store advertised as being open 24 hours but the doors were closed and locked. Turman noticed an old man sweeping the aisles and motioned for him to unlock the door. The old man shook his head no and moved out of Turman's sight.

"That ole man in there won't let me in," said Turman as he climbed back into the Buick.

"Ah forget it, I'm getting tired too, let's head out to mothers," suggested Utah.

"Alright," agreed his brother.

The two boys drove out to their mother's 10 acre farm in the Green Mountain area of Camas, Washington. The sun hadn't come up yet but the darkness that surrounded them as they drove was slowly changing into an opaque orangey-red color all around them.

As they approached the property, Turman suddenly stopped the Buick.

"What's wrong with this damn car now?" asked his younger brother.

"Look, see the car parked by Huddleston's Gas Station?"

"Yes."

"And the one over there across the street from ma's driveway?"

"Yea."

"And one more there on the corner?"

"Uh huh, what about 'em?" asked Utah.

"They all got double aerials on 'em and look at the license plates they're cops!"

"Oh no! I bet they want to take me in on account of that stolen power saw, what should we do Turm?"

"We need to change cars. Let's go get your Pontiac from Grant."

"Okay, let's get out of here," Utah quickly agreed.

The sun was peeking over Mt. Hood when Turman pulled his Buick in back of Utah's Pontiac at Grants Wilson's house. Grant was up drinking a cup of coffee and getting ready for work when he saw the black Buick pull up to his house.

"Where have you been?" asked Grant opening his front door for Turman and Utah to enter.

"We went to see Dad in Silverton."

"What for?" questioned Grant.

"Remember when Utah did some bucking and sawing up on Larch Mountain?"

"Yea," answered Grant.

"Well, I guess a power saw has come up missing and the police want to pick up Utah for it."

"Oh no," lamented Grant, "what did Dad say?"

"He wasn't much help."

"Maybe you should go out to Mother's."

"We've already been out there. After the picture show was out Utah was going to drop me off before heading over to Lucille's apartment but there were cops out front."

"How'd you know that?"

"Cause the cars me and Utah saw had double aerials on 'em."

"So where'd you go?" asked Grant.

"Well, when we saw the cops we didn't want to stop, so we came by your house to get Utah's Pontiac."

The boy's older brother informed them that he had to get to work so the three brothers made plans to meet each other again during Grant's lunch break from work.

It was around the sixth hour of the morning on Monday, March 20th when Turman and Utah drove off to Lacamas Lake while Grant headed for the Crown Zellerback Paper Mill. The boys stopped at the Lacamas Lake Grocery Store and purchased some wieners, buns, mustard, cupcakes and milk. Then they drove to a public park located beside the lake and started a small campfire. A wispy trail of white smoke rose up through the early morning mist coming off of the lake as the boy's wieners sizzled in the hot flames of the fire. With full stomachs, the boys got drowsy. Turman laid down in the front seat and Utah in the back seat where they slept until it was time to meet their brother.

Grant agreed to meet his brothers that afternoon in the Black Forest. The Black Forest wasn't an official name for the area around Lacamas Lake but the locals had dubbed it that and it truly lived up to it's name. Tall Washington State Evergreen trees so thick you couldn't see the sky above you. Not even at high noon could the tiniest ray of sunshine penetrate the pitchy branches thick with pine needles. This made the narrow road going through the Black Forest like a tunnel. Grant had the headlights on in the Pontiac as he approached Turman's Buick parked on the side of the road. Turman and Utah were sitting in the front seat of the car waiting for him.

"Do you want me to go with you guys to the police station and find out what's going on?" asked Grant as the three of them stood outside their cars to talk.

"No!" declared Utah in an uncharacteristic display of authority, "I was told by this lawyer I had once that if the police are ever looking for you, never go to them first, let the police come to you, so I ain't going nowhere near downtown Vancouver."

"I think we should go find Utah some work out of state like his parole officer told him. If he finds work somewhere else he can leave Washington State," said Turman.

"But the Buick's not running good, Turm," said Utah as Grant listened.

"We can go to Portland, drop off the car to be fixed and then see about some new insurance," said Turman.

"That sounds like a good idea, you two do that while I head back to work," Grant told them.

"Alright but I'm supposed to be at the woolen mill at four today," said Turman.

"I'll call the mill for you?" offered Grant.

"Ok, I'd like for them to be able to find a replacement for me as soon as possible also tell them if

I'm not back by Thursday to hire someone else for the job."

"You think you'll be gone that long?" asked Grant.

"I don't know how long it's going to take to find Utah a job but I'm going to do all I can to see that he doesn't break his parole and that he stays out of the pen. Plus we was thinking him and Lucille never got a real honeymoon back in December when they got married so we need to fix that with a nice little getaway for them in Portland."

After their Monday afternoon meeting with Grant, Turman and Utah headed back across the Columbia River to take the old Buick to the Broadway One-Stop Service Station in Portland, Oregon. While the car was being worked on they went to Sears to see about car insurance and then took in a movie. Later that evening after the Buick was finished being serviced and running a little better they switched to driving Utah's Pontiac and headed to Vancouver to surprise his wife with the news of a real honeymoon in Portland.

At 10:00 PM on Monday, March 20, 1950 Turman, Utah and his teenage bride Lucille arrived at the Morrison Hotel in downtown Portland, Oregon. The bottom floor of the Morrison Hotel was a jewelry store so they had to walk up a flight of stairs to get to the front desk. In the lobby, the front desk was behind a wall with a sliding glass window. Through the window you could see the living quarters of the managers.

The manager of the hotel registered Utah and Lucille to room number 38 and then escorted them to their room. While the manager was taking Utah and Lucille to their room the manager's wife registered Turman into the hotel. He decided to register under an alias because of the missing power saw situation and signed the registration form as Mr. John R. Williams. Then he was taken to room number 24. Later Turman met up with his younger brother and sister-in-law and they went to supper followed by a show. After that they retired to their separate rooms for the evening.

The following morning after breakfast at a diner across the street from the hotel Turman, Utah and Lucille spent the day meandering around the suburbs of Portland and going to movies. Lucille was enjoying her delayed honeymoon immensely.

The next day, they went to the Yellow Cab Car Company and put down a $50 deposit to rent a 1946, four-door, Dodge sedan. Driving the Dodge to Camas they met Grant at home. Upon Turman's request Grant had gone over to his mother's house and got the money his mother was saving for him. He had managed to acquire over one thousand dollars since his release from prison and subsequent employment at the woolen mill.

After getting the money Utah kissed his wife goodbye and left her at Grant's house. Grant got in the car and went back to Portland with his brothers. Still fearful about getting picked up for a parole violation in the Pontiac, the first thing on their agenda was to purchase a different car. They found an Oldsmobile in a used car lot which Turman paid $245 cash for.

Turman then instructed Grant to abandon the Pontiac on Union Street in Portland. After parking the car, the threesome went back to Green Mountain to their mother's house. The boys said their good-byes and headed for southern Oregon to find Utah a job.

While in Oregon Utah tried procuring employment at a dairy farm and at a couple different laundries but Utah became lonesome for his wife. So the boys decided to head north once again and pulled into Camas, Washington on Friday evening March 24, 1950. Every available man in the Clark County area was called on to comb the county in a supreme, all-out effort to find Jo Ann Dewey. After days of fruitless effort on the part of law enforcement agencies in two states to solve the case of Jo Ann's abduction Sunday night, a conference was called of local law enforcement heads, Police Chief Harry Diamond, Sheriff Earl Anderson and State Patrol Sergeant James Coshow. In addition to volunteers Mayor Vern Anderson planned to contact the saddle clubs in the county to solicit their aid in the search. Officials further requested that people throughout the county search their own premises thoroughly.

Did the Wilson's search their own premises for someone none of them had ever heard of? Maybe they searched, maybe they didn't but one thing the family decided on that Friday night before the organized search began the following Saturday was that Utah's freedom was top priority. Since there were no jobs in Oregon they decided to try finding migrant work in California. The hope was to get Utah a job and have him stay there until the next meeting with his parole officer in April.

After spending the weekend with his wife and while the biggest missing person's search Washington State had ever seen was taking place Utah left for California with his older brother on Monday March 27th, 1950. On Tuesday the boys crossed the Oregon-California border and checked into a motel. They washed, had supper and then took in a movie before heading back to their rooms and retiring for the evening to get some sleep.

On Wednesday they had made it as far as Sacramento when they decided to see if that city had any job openings. Turman wanted to make sure the car insurance he recently purchased was in effect so he called his brother Grant from his hotel room.

CHAPTER SEVEN

"SACRAMENTO"

Grant Wilson was 22 years old, responsible and dependable. He was labeled as a "good Christian man from start to finish." His brothers looked up to him as a person who never did anything wrong. After Turman called him from Sacramento he couldn't sleep that night. There was something gnawing at his conscience that he couldn't shake. He got up out of bed and called Reverend Ralph Cranston, the leader of his local church.

The two agreed to meet at the Reverend's house. When Grant arrived the Reverend had coffee ready and they sat across from each other at the dining room table. After a short conversation about the telephone call from Turman in Sacramento, Reverend Cranston decided it was best to call the police.

Within approximately 20 minutes Detective's Borgan and Ulmer of the Vancouver Police department were at the home of Reverend Ralph Cranston. Grant Wilson told them everything he knew about his brother's activities. The detectives grilled Grant incessantly going over every detail of his brother's activities including their whereabouts. Finally the two officers left Reverend Cranston's house and went to the Vancouver police station. There at the station with Police Chief Harry Diamond the three of them rolled up their sleeves, put on a strong pot of coffee and got busy building a case against the Wilson's. After hours of unbroken labor on Thursday, March 30, 1950 first-degree murder and first degree kidnapping warrants were issued for Turman and Utah Wilson. The warrants were issued from the Clark county prosecutor's office. When the prosecutor issued the warrants he also held a press conference and gave the following statement to The Columbian newspaper:

> *"Because of the records of the Wilson brothers, the officers gave close attention to their whereabouts from the night the crime was committed. An old model Pontiac, found in Portland yesterday was established as the one driven by the two brothers and it answered the general description given by the witnesses. Human blood was found on the floor of this car. There is no indications that the abductors of the Dewey girl were seeking her specifically. The men were perhaps waiting for the nurses to come off duty, knowing that the street was dark and hoping that they might grab one of the young women who might come out alone. I praise the*

*police department for the fine job they
have done on this case, they have left no
stone unturned in tracing possible clues.
The officers have now developed a prima
facie case against these two on both
counts. The evidence against the boys
should be sufficient to draw the death
penalty".*

Over 600 miles away, the Wilson brothers were
watching a picture show in Sacramento, California.
The car they drove down to the California State Capital
was a 1938 Oldsmobile five-passenger coupe with an
Oregon license plate. At the time the car was spotted
by the law, it was parked and vacant. Within a couple
of hours, five FBI agents and four Sacramento police
officers had assembled near where the car was parked.
They drafted a plan to apprehend the pair when they
returned to the car.

It was dusk when the movie got over. The boys
naturally returned to their car. Turman sensed
something wasn't right. Just as he went to put the car
key in the lock, armed men surrounded him and his
brother. Facing a shotgun and drawn revolvers pointed
at their chests the boys didn't offer any resistance.
They were taken to the local county jail in Sacramento.
They were searched and booked, then confined and
interrogated separately. Later their bail was set at
$25,000 each.

Utah assumed the interrogation was going to be
about the missing power saw and his parole violation

when he was captured. Three FBI agents took him into the office of the Assistant Chief of Police and questioned him extensively on things that puzzled him. Turman's questioning lasted only one hour. Without legal counsel he chose to exercise his Fifth Amendment Right by not speaking so as not to incriminate himself.

On Friday, March 31, 1950, 24 hours after the Wilson brothers were arrested the first news interview was granted. It was stipulated by the authorities at the jail that the boys be interviewed separately. The older Wilson brother was questioned first.

"Why'd you come to California?" came the first question as camera light bulbs popped and flashed.

"I wanted to watch over my younger brother."

"Aren't you really here to escape prosecution?"

"No, Utah is on parole and I knew leaving the state would be a violation of his parole. I came along 'cause he wanted to light out of Washington 'cause a power saw came up missing and he knew the Vancouver Police would finger him for it."

"Were you at the Vancouver bus depot on the night of March 19th?"

"No, I seldom go near Vancouver, the police there haven't got a liking for me, anything happens up there in Washington they accuse me."

"What kind of beer do you drink?"

"I don't drink much beer."

"What about your brother?"

"He drinks occasionally."

"Did you know the police found a beer bottle with your brother's fingerprints on it at the scene of the crime?"

"What are you talking about? I have no idea what you're talking about, me and my brother was picked up for a parole violation."

"What do you think of your brother Grant turning you in?"

"Grant's never done a wrong thing in his life."

After about twenty minutes the news interview was over and Turman was returned to his cell. The same questions were asked of Utah and shortly thereafter he too was returned to his own cell separate from his older brother.

The following day April 1, 1950, Vancouver Detectives Borgan and Ulmer were in Sacramento. They had Utah alone until noon. During this time they played the classic game of "Good Cop/Bad Cop" except with a little twist, they played "Bad Cop/Worse Cop". Ulmer swore at the youngster profusely using profanity that would make a sow blush. Borgan told Utah he had the power to release his father's 1933 criminal record of incest with Utah's sister to the press. He assured Utah this information would cause the public to go out and string his folks up.

After lunch Turman received much the same treatment from the two detectives. However he was used to this kind of treatment from the law and it didn't affect him as much as it did Utah.

On Sunday, April 2, the head of the Vancouver investigation, Sheriff Earl Anderson and his deputy arrived in Sacramento. They checked into the Senator Hotel where they met with Detectives Borgan, Ulmer and Chief Diamond. The five of them then went to the jail for more interrogation of their prisoners. Afterwards they returned to the hotel where they had drinks and dinner together.

Over dinner they discussed Turman's refusal to sign extradition papers and decided to call the prosecuting attorney in Vancouver. From his hotel room, Sheriff Anderson got the prosecuting attorney's advice, "Well, it looks like we are going to be here for awhile," said the sheriff to his comrades as he hung up the phone, "Word is, it's going to take several days for the extradition paperwork to get here."

Utah was homesick for his wife, mother and brother and finally gave in and signed the extradition papers. Turman was still unwilling to sign his papers but once he learned Utah had signed the waiver he too gave in because he wanted to be able to look after his little brother on the long journey home.

It was a sunny California afternoon when the little legal posse from Vancouver had their two charges in tow. Police Chief Diamond, Sheriff Anderson and Detective Borgan rode in one car with Utah while Deputy Scott and Detective Ulmer rode with Turman. The entourage arrived in Klamath Falls, Oregon at midnight. Arrangements were made at the local jail for Turman to be upstairs in the felony tier with other prisoners while Utah was isolated in a cell downstairs.

Before the troupe left the Klamath Falls jail the following morning, Police Chief Diamond and

Detective Borgan hatched a creative little side trip especially for the younger Wilson brother. At ten o'clock in the morning they handcuffed Utah and put the "Oregon Boot" on him. The Oregon Boot was a handcuff for the ankles with a short three inch bar in the middle. Then they loaded him into the police car. The side trip started after they crossed the "Bridge of the Gods" out of Oregon and into Washington State. From there the police car with Utah in it followed the main highway into Carson, Washington. Shackled in the Oregon Boot, separated from his brother and sitting beside a man who hated his guts Utah had no idea what was going to happen to him. The officers drove him down an old country road that had a steep cliff on one side. The road they were driving on was referred to as "Carson Road" and it led into the Wind River Canyon where Jo Ann Dewey's body was found.

Police Chief Diamond picked a spot by a footbridge alongside the Wind River to stop the car. Diamond and Borgan got out of the car and walked out onto the bridge. They smoked a couple of cigarettes and kicked rocks off the suspension bridge into the raging Wind River below them. Utah was older and bigger than the little eight-year-old Propagator who was dangled over the same Wind River by her father earlier that same year and threatened with death if she told what she saw happen to Jo Ann Dewey but just as helpless while handcuffed and shackled in the boot Utah was in an extreme state of fear not wanting to move a muscle or even breath. When they thought

Utah had enough they got back in the car and resumed the drive to Vancouver, Washington.

A crowd of about 30 people including the boy's mother, Grant Wilson, spectators, reporters and photographers had gathered at the Clark County sheriff's office in Vancouver to meet the cavalcade. Police Chief Diamond decided to change the groups itinerary at the last minute because he thought there might be a "crackpot" with a gun seated in one of the nearby parked cars.

Sheriff Anderson agreed with the Police Chief who told reporters in a quote that they, "Did not wish to take a chance of having trouble when the prisoners were brought in, inasmuch as the protection of the brothers was their responsibility we also have a responsibility to protect all citizens. The brothers will be brought to Vancouver without prior notice because a crowd is not wanted."

The boys were then expedited to the Cowlitz County jail in Kelso, Washington. This was an additional 40 mile drive North of Vancouver. Tired from the long trip and not knowing what was happening to his younger brother, Turman lost his temper and exploded in his cell.

"This is a false arrest!" He yelled, grabbing the bars and trying to shake them, "I'm going to sue everyone here! Do you hear me? I mean it! I'll sue all you all!"

It was Wednesday, April 5, 1950, when the Wilson's long journey from Sacramento to the Clark County jail in Vancouver, Washington ended. After being stripped of their street clothes, they were attired in the standard prison uniform of white coveralls with a big-zippered front. Then came an interview with waiting news reporters. Anyone related to the Wilson's was put in the spotlight by the press. This included Utah's young bride, Lucille Wilson. The 91 pound brunette was embroidering on a bright piece of cloth in her mother's apartment on the evening of her first interview with the news reporter.

"Utah was trying to straighten up and they wouldn't give him a chance," she began defensively as the questioning began, "I don't care what happens around here, the law will always go after the Wilson's. Another person could have done it, someone without a record even but as soon as it happened they started after the Wilson's again," close to tears, she continued venting her feelings to the listening ear of the reporter, "Utah and I wanted to leave Washington after we were married last December but couldn't because of his parole. We just want to be left alone and allowed to live our own lives, like other people," she commented hopefully, "I know Utah well enough to know when he is under a strain or has something on his mind and I can tell immediately when he is lying. If he had anything to do with that dreadful act he would have shown it in his actions, I know he would have, but he was completely normal in every way," she insisted.

"In fact, about two weeks ago Utah came home in a nervous state because he had run over a dog on the highway. He put the dog in his car and took it to the vet. That night after we had gone to bed Utah couldn't sleep. He said he couldn't get that dog's suffering face out of his mind. If he acted that way over a dog, what do you think he'd do after killing a girl as they are trying to say he did?" she inquired, "The newspapers state all the bad things and none of the good about my husband and his brother," she concluded.

The next day during a news session a reporter told Utah that his wife had said that she believed in him and would stand by him. This produced a spark of life in Utah as he smiled broadly and remarked that he wanted to see his wife and mother first before anyone else.

CHAPTER EIGHT

"THE TRIAL BEGINS"

The Washington State Regional Archives System began a program to make public records available in the geographic regions where they were created. Records of personal and community history formerly kept only at the capital were now being stored closer to where the general public could have access to court cases, maps, plats and ledgers. The entire transcript of over 1200 pages of "State of Washington VS Turman Wilson and Utah Wilson" was stored in just such a place for just such a time as this to be revealed. The raw material of the court recorded trial transcript has been condensed and written into a parable format with descriptive narrative for ease of reading and better understandability.

Irvin Goodman of "Goodman & Levenson's Attorney's and Counselors at Law", in Portland, Oregon was middle aged, short and carried a few extra pounds on his stubby frame. He had dark hair with a pointed receding hairline and a long narrow face.

Goodman spent four days questioning Turman and Utah Wilson. He finally made a decision as to whether or not he would represent the Wilson brothers on Monday April 10, 1950. In a statement he released to the public he said;

> *"On Friday March 31, Mrs. Eunice Wilson, her son Grant, and Reverend Cranston of Camas called my office and requested I represent Turman and Utah. I advised them I was unable to decide because of prior legal commitments and also because I first wanted to interview the boys and be convinced of the facts. They returned to my office the following Monday and in their presence I telephoned Sacramento to advise the boys to waive extradition.*
>
> *I have decided to defend Turman and Utah, that is, with permission of the court since I am an Oregon lawyer. Obviously, this decision bears a heavy responsibility but one of a lawyer's duties. One that has been a guiding principle with me throughout my practice of law is never to reject for any reason the cause of the defenseless or the oppressed.*
>
> *I have represented Turman on one prior occasion. He had been indicted for the crime of assault and robbery, being armed with a dangerous*

weapon. He told me he was innocent and that 'once a fellow has done time the police just don't leave you alone.'

After more than 15 hours of exhaustive interrogation, with documentary evidence I have procured and because of my past acquaintance with them, I have no reason to doubt the boy's word that they are absolutely innocent. Therefore, upon the basis of my present information, I believe the perpetrators of the crime are still at large.

I hope the law enforcement officers are exploring all clues and that they are not losing valuable time by awaiting the outcome of the trial.

The newspapers have reported that the Wilson brothers have been high on their list of suspects for several days, but what efforts are being made to apprehend other suspects?

During my interviews, the boys expressed concern over a statement about their mother that appeared in the newspapers. It stated that Mrs. Eunice Wilson was given a ten-year suspended sentence for harboring an escaped criminal. What disturbed them was that the statement did not mention the escaped criminal was her own son who returned home after he fled from the Oregon State Penitentiary.

There are many questions in the public mind concerning this case, questions that could be asked of both prosecution and defense. This case is too serious to speculate about and without further information I must reserve any further comment at this time.

It is fundamental that the presumption of innocence applies to every person accused of crime until guilt is established beyond a reasonable doubt. These boys like all Americans are entitled to that presumption and to a trial before a fair and impartial jury in accordance with established legal procedure. Turman and Utah believe they will receive such a trial."

Shortly after the release of this statement all the key players gathered together in the Clark County courtroom for the arraignment. Turman wore a gray, pinstriped suit with a yellow and red striped tie, while Utah was dressed in a white collared dress shirt, dark blue suit with a light blue tie. They sat quietly at the defense table beside their two attorneys Irvin Goodman and Sanford Clement. Both boys sat attentively with their hands folded in their laps.

Sanford Clement was the Washington State appointed attorney for the Wilsons. He was 36 years old, with Perry Mason-like facial features. He was big boned and was the best-dressed lawyer in the courtroom. On arraignment day he wore a dark tailored suit, new crisp white collared dress shirt and had a white, linen handkerchief extending from his suit pocket.

At the opposing table in the room was the prosecuting attorney R. DeWitt Jones. He was 41 years old. He would use all means necessary not to lose a case and he didn't like to work with Oregon lawyers.

The State of Washington randomly selected 63 registered voters who were whittled down to 12 jurors. They were to report for jury duty at 9:00 AM sharp on June 12, 1950.

On that warm summer morning at precisely 9:00, Judge Eugene Cushing was regally dressed in his robe and collared shirt as he entered the packed courtroom. He had thick dark hair, big ears, thin lips and a straight, long nose but his ballast feature was his doe-like, wide-set eyes which were framed beautifully in manicured brows. He was a family man and served as Judge Advocate with the New Orleans Port of Embarkation where upon being relieved of active duty he returned to Vancouver, Washington in December of 1945 and went on the bench a month later. He was re-elected to office in 1946 for a two-year term and again in 1948 for a four-year term. He was a strict judge who didn't allow standing spectators in his courtroom. After the seats were filled the doors were closed and guarded by the bailiff. The courtroom could only seat 75 people comfortably but when squished together, the bailiff did his best to seat almost a hundred people every day. The unlucky people who didn't get to court early enough to get a seat, waited outside in the hall, hoping for someone to give up their seat at the noon recess, but people who were fortunate enough to get a seat in the morning brought sack lunches for the noon recess and stayed to the end of the day.

Judge Cushing excluded all witnesses from the courtroom until they were called upon to testify. They waited out in the hall with the overflow until summoned by the bailiff.

The trial was officially kicked off after a field trip to the crime scene. Next the opening statements were made and finally the first witnesses were called. They were the Central Court Apartment residents. Each and every person testified to hearing blood-curdling screams, and seeing a large, dark-colored, high-powered car drive away into the darkness on Sunday night, March 19, 1950.

Following the apartment witnesses, Vancouver policemen were called in to testify. Officers Edmonds and Perry recalled how they were on the scene first and found Jo Ann's purse strap, gold hairpin and a blood spot about two inches in diameter.

When Sergeant Forsbeck, also known as "Buck", took the stand he told how he adamantly searched the area for tire tracks of the abduction vehicle. When no tire tracks were found on the concrete streets, he met up with Officer Frank Irvin who was talking with the apartment witnesses. Then they drove back to the scene of the abduction and there in the middle of the street was a beer bottle.

Buck told how he, "tipped the beer out of it" he also noticed large bubbles in the bottle as he was pouring the evidence onto the street.

After Prosecuting Attorney Jones questioned Buck, the court took its first recess. Buck was recalled to the stand and cross-examined by Defense Attorney Goodman when court resumed session at 1:30 PM. The judge informed Buck that he was still under oath as he took the stand and the questioning began.

"What time did you arrive at the scene of the crime?" questioned Goodman.

"Shortly after the call was given us. I think within a minute or two," answered Buck.

"What time was that?"

"The call was 11:38 PM."

"You arrived there when?"

"Within a couple of minutes."

"Around 11:40 PM?"

"Around that, pretty close."

"After you arrived, the abduction car and the occupants had already gone had they not?"

"Correct."

"Then upon your investigation, Sergeant Forsbeck, at the scene of the crime you observed, as you testified this morning, a beer bottle which was marked for identification as Plaintiff's exhibit nine?"

"Yes, sir."

"Do you know how many people were present at the time that you arrived at the scene of the crime?"

"I don't know, there were several people there, I didn't count them."

"Could you estimate the number?'

"Well, I would say five or six, anyway, something like that, possibly more."

"Five or six?" questioned Goodman in a higher tone and with a raised eyebrow.

"That is in front of the apartment house entrance," elaborated Buck.

"What I'm referring to and endeavoring to find out from you is how many people were present at the scene of the crime at the time that you found the beer bottle, or in that immediate vicinity?"

"There was two at the scene of the crime."

"Pardon?"

"Two," repeated Buck.

"Speak a little louder," requested Goodman.

"Myself and Officer Irvin when I picked up the bottle."

"Who?"

"Officer Irvin."

"Officer Irvin and you were present when you picked up the bottle?"

"Correct."

"First, how many other people were present in this immediate vicinity except you and Officer Irvin?"

"None that I know of."

"You don't know how many people were present at the scene of the crime?"

"I object!" said Jones as he jumped to his feet, "that is obviously foolish."

"Strike the question," responded Goodman as he continued questioning the Vancouver police sergeant, "of course the beer bottle arrived at the scene of the crime before you did?"

"Yes sir."

"The beer bottle was there before you got there wasn't it?"

"Yes."

"Who was there first, you or the beer bottle?" questioned Goodman as laughter ensued from the audience.

"I object to the form of the question as being improper," interjected Jones.

"Sustain the objection;" said Judge Cushing with a quick rap of his gavel, "I want to caution the people in the courtroom we will have no demonstrations. If we do I will clear the courtroom. Let's have that understood. Mr. Goodman is trying this case and Mr. Jones is trying this case and they will have no interference, proceed Mr. Goodman."

"Do you have any information of your own personal knowledge how long the beer bottle was there before you arrived?"

"No."

"No further cross-examination," concluded Goodman.

"You may call your next witness," said Judge Cushing.

Jones rose to his feet as he glanced down at his witness list on the table in front of him.

"The state calls Officer Frank Irvin to the stand."

Having been sworn in by the bailiff, the policeman testified as the prosecutor questioned him.

"What is your occupation?"

"Patrolman, Vancouver Police."

"Were you on patrol duty on March 19th around 11:30 at night?"

"Yes, sir."

"Is Sergeant Forsbeck your partner?"

"No, he usually stays at the station."

"Where were you when the call came in?"

"I had just stopped at the station to pick up my original partner."

"When Sergeant Forsbeck got in your car what route did you take?"

"Immediately we went down Washington to 12th and then East to D Street, at that time another car was at that point so I proceeded on North to 13th and D."

"When you got to 13th and D Street, what did you do?" asked Jones.

"I started to cover both sides of the apartments and Sergeant Forsbeck took out on the street."

"You let him out on the corner and you remained in the car?"

"Yes sir."

"And Sergeant Forsbeck went out on the street?"

"Yes."

"And what did you do after you watched both sides of the apartments?"

"As near as I could tell, Sergeant Forsbeck was on his way back and I pulled down to 13th and C Street to pick him up.   He had been to the scene and was coming back."

"Then what did you do?"

"After we searched the area we were sure whatever car was involved made its getaway and we immediately proceeded back to look over the scene a little bit."

"When you arrived at 12th Street between C and D did you stop your car?"

"Yes, we stopped in the middle of the street. We were trying to use the headlights to search the area."

"Did you notice anything up the street?"

"We first noticed a beer bottle and a wet spot around it."

"There were still some bubbles of foam within the bottle?"

"Yes, sir, there were."

"I think that is all," concluded the prosecutor.

Next Attorney Goodman rose from his chair behind the defense table and approached Officer Irvin.

"How long have you been a police officer?"

"Going on five years."

"You have gained some knowledge, of course, during the five year period as to the value of evidence in the trial of a case?"

"Yes sir."

"Why did you men pour out the beer?"

"We didn't think we would need it."

"Beg your pardon?" asked Goodman with eyes raised and an ear tilted towards the witness while facing the jury box.

"I didn't think we would need it."

"In other words, it is your testimony that the beer left in the bottle might not be of evidentiary value in court?"

"At that time I thought it would have no evidentiary value," admitted Officer Irvin.

"Do you frequently find beer bottles out in the street or in the parking strip in the vicinity of the St. Joseph's Hospital?"

"No, a bottle thrown from a car wouldn't stay in the road."

"No further cross-examination, Your Honor."

"Witness is excused," said the judge.

The next Vancouver Police officer to take the stand was Floyd William Borgan. He testified to taking the beer bottle to a fingerprint expert in Portland, named Stanley MacDonald.

Stanley MacDonald was the Superintendent of Identification for the Sheriff's Office in Portland, Oregon. A subpoena was filed and received at the Sheriff's office but MacDonald was hospitalized and the summons was cancelled. After the trial was over and MacDonald had recovered he released the following data to the public at the request of Goodman:

> *"That on or about March 30, 1950, there was received in the Multnomah County Criminal Bureau of Identification, a stubby beer bottle*

bearing the label of an Olympia Brewing Company, without other marks of identification except that it had been treated with a gray latent fingerprint powder.

The bottle had been received from two Vancouver, Washington Police Officers and obviously the impressions had been lifted with scotch tape.

The latent prints upon the bottle were to be checked against those of three suspects but what remained of the details of the latent impressions on the bottle after the lifting process was not sufficient to involve either of the first two subjects.

The following day, a Vancouver Police Officer came into the bureau and requested the return of the bottle, as a result the checking of the bottle against the third suspect, Utah Wilson, was not finished.

Because of the lifting process and the poor quality of what remained of the impressions, I probably would have never been able to have identified them."

Not knowing that this information would be released over a year later, Goodman continued his questioning of Officer Borgan on another subject.

"Did you make the following statement to Utah in Sacramento, that if he didn't confess to the abduction you would have Utah's mother and the rest of the family in jail, and that you could release certain things to the press that could make the public go out to his mother's house and string Utah's folks up?"

"I don't remember anything, any statement like that," answered Borgan.

"You also know Turman Wilson, do you not?" continued the defense attorney.

"I do."

"I will ask you to state whether at the Police Station in Vancouver, Washington in November 1948, you told Turman Wilson if you saw him in town at all you would shoot his legs out from under him?"

"I never made any such statement."

"I will ask you to state whether in the Sacramento Sheriff's office on April 1, 1950 you told Turman Wilson in effect that by the time Sheriff Anderson got down to Sacramento Turman wouldn't know himself in a mirror…"

"I did not, I never made any such statement," interrupted Borgan.

"I am sorry, I didn't finish, 'that Turman would not know himself in a mirror when you got through with him'"?

"I never made any such statement."

"You may take the witness," finished Goodman as he headed back to the defense table and Prosecuting Attorney Jones approached Officer Borgan for more questioning.

"Mr. Borgan, you asked Mr. MacDonald to check the prints on the bottle against some person named?"

"That is right."

"What report did you get from him in connection with that?

"Mr. McDonald said there was no similarity or comparison."

"That is all," concluded Jones.

Next a fingerprint expert from Washington D.C. for the prosecution testified to examining a lift of a fingerprint taken from the beer bottle and sent to him by the Vancouver Police Department. Mr. Goodman objected to the beer bottle being admitted into evidence on the grounds that the fingerprint on the bottle was not that of Utah's, secondly that the bottle itself was not examined and thirdly, that the lift was done by another person as admitted by the witness.

Judge Cushing overruled the objection and the beer bottle was admitted into evidence, whereupon the court adjourned until the following morning.

It was still week one of the sensationalized murder trial when Jo Ann's mother, friends and neighbor took the stand. Mrs. Dewey had returned to Vancouver for the trial from Casper, Wyoming where her husband had started a new job. She was called as a witness for the plaintiff and after having been sworn in the prosecuting attorney started the questioning of the heartbroken woman.

"Would you state your name to the jury please?"

"Anna Eunice Dewey."

"Where do you live, Mrs. Dewey?"

"Well, my home is at Battleground in Meadow Glade but at present we are residing in Casper, Wyoming."

"How long has your home been in the Meadow Glade District near Battleground?"

"Twelve years."

"Where did you reside on March 19th of this year?"

"At Meadow Glade."

"Do you have any children?"

"Yes, I have six children."

"Was Jo Ann Dewey your daughter?"

"Yes, she is my youngest child."

"Where was Jo Ann living on March 19th?"

"She was working at the Portland Sanitarium and lived in the next block, I think, with a friend."

"How old was Jo Ann?"

"Eighteen last October."

"Where was she employed March 19, 1950?"

"The Portland Sanitarium."

"Do you know the kind of work Jo Ann did?"

"She worked in the kitchen as a kitchen-aid."

"Do you know how long she had been employed there?"

"I think five or six weeks."

"Calling your attention to the night of March 19, 1950, did you talk to Jo Ann?"

"I did. She called me up."

"From that conversation do you know where she was?"

"I asked her where she was and she said she was at the Vancouver Bus Depot and called me to see if she could find a way home."

"Where were you?"

"I was in the nursing home and I was on duty until ten o'clock."

"Were you able to find a ride?"

"No we have no phone at our home."

"Did you talk to Jo Ann in connection with where she was to go?"

"I said Jo Ann I guess I can't get any ride and you go to the St. Joseph's Hospital and stay with Mrs. Crull and come out with her the next morning."

"Calling your attention to the following morning, March 20th did Jo Ann arrive at home?"

"She usually stopped where I worked and I didn't quit work until about eight and since she had not stopped I waited for her to stop."

"Did you contact Mrs. Crull?"

"Just as soon as I got away and asked her where Jo Ann was and she said 'I haven't seen her.'"

"After you found from Mrs. Crull that Jo Ann had not contacted her Sunday night, what did you do?"

"I was alarmed immediately. She told us the scream she heard."

Attorney Jones stopped Mrs. Dewey's testimony with an objection to her testifying about the scream Mrs. Crull heard on Sunday night. However attorney Goodman made no objection and stated that Mrs. Dewey could say whatever she desired.

Jones retorted by saying, "We want to keep it under legal evidence," and Mrs. Dewey continued with her answer by saying, "I went to my home hoping that somebody in the Glade had brought her home and I went home and looked in her bed and she had never been there. Then I went to the Vancouver Police Station."

"When you arrived down there, did they show you any items or articles?"

"Yes they did."

"This purse strap, do you recognize that?"

The heartbroken mother had answered the Prosecutor's questions firmly until she was shown her daughter's personal items. Then the rest of her answers came with a bowed head and in a trembling soft voice, "Absolutely, my son had to fix it a week before - it came off at one end."

"To whose purse was this strap attached when you last saw it?"

"Jo Ann."

"This barrette, do you recognize it?"

"Yes, she had two of them."

"Did these belong to your daughter?"

"Yes."

The weeping mother was not cross-examined by Goodman, he said he would make no objection to admitting the murdered girl's barrette and purse strap as evidence and the witness was excused. Next Jo Ann's best friend since the seventh grade took the stand, her name was Joan Crawford.

"What time did Jo Ann get off work on March 19th?" asked the prosecutor.

"Seven o'clock," the witness answered.

"And were you there when she got off work?"

"Yes."

"Where did you go with her that evening?"

"We went to see Samson and Delilah playing at the Paramount."

"When were you out of that show?"

"A little after ten."

"After you got out of the show, where did you go?"

"We went to the bus depot."

"What time was it when you left her at the bus depot?"

"About 10:25 PM."   "Did you ever see Jo Ann again?"

"No."

"How was Jo Ann dressed?"

"She had on a white blouse and blue skirt and bobby socks. She also had on a full-length cocoa brown outer coat."

"I am showing you now a piece of cloth which is in the form of a belt know as Identification 13 in this matter. Will you look at that and state whether or not you have ever seen it before or if you can recognize it in connection with the clothing she was wearing?"

"This is the same color as the coat she had."

"Was the coat of that same material?"

"Yes gabardine."

"What property did Jo Ann have on her possession when you left her?"

"She had a leather shopping bag with some clothes she was taking home that needed washing and she had her black plastic purse."

After returning the evidence to the Evidence Table in the courtroom, the prosecutor continued questioning Miss Crawford.

"Did you see Jo Ann buy her bus ticket?"

"Yes."

"Did she have any money in her purse?"

"She had a little."

"Who paid for the tickets to the show?"

"I did."

"Did you observe her when she bought her ticket to Vancouver?"

"Yes."

"Did she have any money at that time?"

"Uh huh, some change."

"That's all," finished Attorney Jones and without any cross examination by the defense attorney, Joan Crawford stepped down from the witness box dabbing tears from her eyes with her handkerchief.

The court took its noon recess after other friends and neighbors recounted their versions of the last hours of Jo Ann's life. When the court reconvened at 1:30 that afternoon Grant Wilson took the stand for the prosecution.

Grant was the younger brother of Turman and the older brother of Utah. He was slow of speech and was on the witness stand for three grueling hours of questioning. At times Grant was calm and in other instances his testimony was halting, it was very apparent he was nervous. He stated with great sincerity that at no time did he believe that his brothers were hiding out because of the abduction of a girl that his brothers never even knew. He stated that they were keeping out of sight because they thought Utah was wanted by the police in connection with the theft of a power saw. He recalled the conversation he had with his two brothers over the prospect of coming back to Vancouver by April 10th, the date Utah was scheduled to report to his parole officer, Frank O'Brien. All three of the brothers agreed that O'Brien was a fair man and would help their younger brother get his parole situation straightened out.

The main questions for Grant were in regards to the family cars. He testified that the three cars had been kept in his name so that if Turman and Utah got in trouble with the police the finance company couldn't confiscate the vehicles, which would result in the brothers losing the money they had paid on them. Grant described the trunk on the back of the Buick car at Goodman's request, stating that "it was not very big." He also stated that a spare tire was kept inside together with a wooden box and a can for gas in case they ran out. The trunk had a partition in it. Jones referred to the third car, the 1937 Chevrolet in redirect exam. Grant agreed in answer to the prosecuting attorney that the trunk on this auto was "quite a bit larger" than that on the Buick.

His testimony finally ended after the prosecutor asked him if he had ever fished the Wind River with his brothers. Grant testified that he had never fished there with his brothers. He was excused and the court recessed.

CHAPTER NINE

"TRIAL WEEK TWO"

Two superior court jury trials were under way at the same time the Wilson murder case was being held in Judge Eugene Cushing's courtroom. The case was originally scheduled for only one week and as it entered the second week of deliberation other judges were taking cases originally assigned to Cushing.

Turman continued to show up for court neatly suited with a tie. After a long week however, Utah was growing weary and decided to change his clothing attire to more comfortable slacks and a sport shirt.

On Monday morning, June 19, 1950, Judge Cushing had the prosecuting attorney call his first witness of the day. It was Mrs. Nelson, a resident from the Central Court Apartments. She testified to hearing some loud screams as she was reading the paper in bed, then looked out her window and saw a man hitting a woman with his fists.

"After you had observed this woman on the ground and this man striking her did you see anyone else?" asked the prosecutor.

"Yes, sir, a second man came out of the car and started to beat the girl too."

"What did you do?"

"I jumped out of bed and ran to the telephone and called the police."

"Now, you say you saw the first man who was there. Just tell the jury what portion of the man, physically, you could observe and what his position was with reference to the position you observed him in and beating the girl."

"I could see he was of medium build and dark hair and dark clothing on."

"Did you see the other man's clothing?"

"He had light clothing, a hat and light colored jacket."

"After this happened did you observe any pictures that appeared in the papers in connection with this matter?"

"Just a moment," interjected Goodman, "I object to that question as hearsay and move the question and answer be stricken and the court so instructs the jury."

"Mr. Goodman's motion is granted and the jury is instructed to disregard from your mind the question and answer," ruled Judge Cushing.

"Mrs. Nelson," continued the prosecutor, "did you at anytime come to the County Jail and observe a lineup of men?"

"Yes I did."

"When was that?"

"That was a couple months ago in April."

"From the observations you made that night you pointed out two men that you felt were similar?"

"They had similar appearance to what I had seen, yes."

"Going back to the observations which you made out of your window, what part of the men's physical makeup did you observe?"

"The man I saw bending over the girl had dark hair and he was the larger of the two and he was the one beating the girl."

"You observed he had dark hair," reiterated the prosecutor, "did you observe any other physical characteristics about him?"

"None, other than he was medium-build."

"Did you ever see his face?"

"No."

"What about the second man, did you observe his face?"

"No, he more or less had his face down as he was running."

"I think that is all," concluded Jones.

"Mrs. Nelson," addressed Defense Attorney Goodman as he approached the witness, "you were pretty sleepy when you made all of these observations, you had just gone to bed?"

"Yes, but I wasn't asleep."

"What time was it when you made these observations?"

"It was around 11:30 PM."

"On the night in question, March 19, 1950, you retired about what time?"

"About 11:15 PM."

"You were pretty sleepy at that time?"

"No."

"Why did you go to bed then?" asked Goodman as the courtroom erupted in laughter.

"If the Court please," said Prosecutor Jones angrily from behind the prosecution's table, "I don't think we should have any demonstration from any people sitting here about questions and answers and I object to the question as being argumentative."

"I will sustain counsel's objection. I also wish to caution the people in the courtroom not to make any comment in any way or any demonstrations in any manner. Otherwise I will clear the courtroom, proceed Mr. Goodman."

"About how far away from the abduction would you say you were when you looked out of your apartment window?"

"I don't know."

"How long did you continue to look out the window?"

"Just a couple of minutes."

"So, after you looked out the window a couple of minutes what did you do?"

"I didn't look out the window a couple of minutes, I just barely glanced out the window and was knocking."

"You barely glanced out the window, how long did you look out the window altogether in question?"

"It wasn't over three minutes."

"Nothing further," concluded Goodman and the witness was excused.

After the noon break the high point of the day's trial came when pathologist, Dr. Howard Richardson took the stand. Dr. Richardson was the Assistant Professor of Pathology at the University of Oregon Medical School where he held a teaching position. His resume' also included being the Director of the Crime Lab of the Oregon State Police. He graduated from medical school in 1940 and took his pre-med training at the College of Puget Sound where he graduated with a degree in Chemistry. He was licensed to practice medicine in Oregon, Washington and California. In the army Dr. Richardson did four autopsies a day for two months straight on Japanese and American soldiers whom died in prison camps.

"When did you first see the body identified as Jo Ann Dewey?" asked the prosecutor as he approached the doctor who had been sworn in and seated in the witness box.

"I first observed the body as being Jo Ann Dewey at 8:00 PM on the 26th day of March, 1950, at the Evergreen Mortuary here in Vancouver, Washington. The body was that of a white female, weighing 170 pounds, very muscular in nature. As I first saw the body I noted the external appearance and wounds. I then proceeded to dictate in detail the sections where the wounds were located and spent an hour photographing these multiple wounds that were present over the body."

"Doctor, did you make color photographs?"

"I made nine in color to demonstrate the color of the body and to demonstrate the exudation of the blood."

"Doctor, would you demonstrate to the jury the wounds you observed on Jo Ann Dewey at the time you performed the autopsy using the pictures?"

The Doctor's photographs had been set up for him earlier that morning by the bailiff. He addressed the men and women in the jury box as he stepped off the witness stand and walked over to an easel to continue his fascinating testimony.

"Those wounds made before death were the wounds under the chin, the upper part of the lips and a wound in back of the right ear," said the doctor as he used a pointer to show the portion of the photograph he referred to, "from the wound in back of the right ear blood continued to drip. In the mouth the teeth were fractured. The left upper incisors were fractured and one of the incisors could actually be taken out and put back in the socket. The lower teeth had been fractured with the teeth broken off. The skin above the right eyebrow was split with abrasions.

Now, the remainder of the marks were made after the death of the individual. Starting with the splitting of the scalp that measured five inches in length," pointed out the pathologist as he continued to show the jury each and every picture admitted into evidence, "the other was a diagonal opening on the left side of the scalp that split through to the bone, but there was no fracture of the skull bones at all."

As Dr. Richardson showed the last picture to the jury he walked back to the witness stand and sat down.

"What other examination of this body did you make with respect to determining the cause of death?" asked Jones.

"Well, the entire body was carefully examined in the beginning. When I first started the examination I removed from the head various fragments of hair from the front and back and various areas, the hair was rather short, four or five inches in length. It was medium brown type hair in color, with one out of every ten hairs in color being jet black.

I then proceeded to examine the hands and they were of a pinkish-purple color. The skin of the hands appeared to be those of a typical washwoman's hands.

The chest was examined externally. I didn't find any markings about it except mottling. The abdomen was examined and the only mark about the abdomen was a puncture mark over the left hip, which was diagonal in nature."

The courtroom was spellbound as the spectators, reporters and jurors were being painted a mental picture of female body parts which nobody talked openly about in 1950.

"The pubic hairs were examined and showed nothing except they had been cut," continued the doctor, "with the ones around the labia especially removed." At the mention of pubic hairs the courtroom was hushed into immediate silence as the Doctor continued his report.

"I examined the external vagina and it showed no evidence of bruises and no evidence of the skin underneath being discolored. I examined the rectum and it was open. It was almost a one-inch opening. I examined it for bruises and evidence of blood in the mucous and there wasn't any."

"What do you mean?" asked the prosecutor.

"Well, I examined the rectal area for any evidence of bruising to see if there was any resistance before death against penetration. There was no evidence of bloody bruises in that area, this penetration was not made before death," a unified gasp of shock and disbelief came from people in the courtroom audience as the pathologist continued undaunted, "the legs, the right foot and the right forearm all had been cut after death. The body was cut as if someone were performing a post-mortem examination.

The lungs, heart, abdomen and uterus were all normal and in their right positions. In the stomach there was a residual of a meal present, this meal was in the stages of digestion and could be followed clear through the small bowel to the large bowel.

Next the skull cap was removed and the brain was exposed, there were two little areas of hemorrhage, then at the base of the brain, there was a considerable amount of hemorrhage. The blow or the trauma exerted to the chin must have been of severe intensity to produce this type of basal injury at the base of the brain. It was a small hemorrhage but not to be interpreted as the cause of death, but may produce unconsciousness of the individual."

"Dr. Richardson, what is your opinion and conclusion for the cause of death to Jo Ann Dewey?"

"The cause of death, I think, after ruling out the blows to the head and her other injuries, the amount of carbon monoxide was sufficient to cause her death."

"Have you handled any cases involving carbon monoxide poisoning?"

"Many cases, it is one of the most peculiar types of death. There are extreme variations in it. There is a variation in the individuals themselves, some individuals are more sensitive to carbon monoxide than others."

"Does weakened resistance, Doctor, have any significance with reference to carbon monoxide poisoning?"

"It could. You could take this room and put carbon monoxide in here and certain people would die and others would live."

Editor's note: because details of her murder were not disclosed in the courtroom this was the reported cause of death.

"Doctor, you made some observations of the skin of the body of Jo Ann Dewey, will you tell what your findings were with reference to the state of preservation?"

"The body was in an excellent state of preservation. It was in so much better state than bodies that have been embalmed by the undertaker. It was just as though the body had been placed in an ice refrigerator and kept some time. It was so good that you might call it a well-preserved body. Goose pimples were still in a state of preservation indicating to me a sudden cooling of a warm body."

The prosecutor changed the subject and continued his questioning of Dr. Richardson.

"I call your attention to a cream colored Pontiac. Did you do some laboratory examination with respect to that?"

"I examined a cream colored Pontiac and a black Buick sedan."

"Did you remove from these vehicles any items or articles for study and examination?"

"I myself scraped the floorboards and removed some of the floor matting. I removed fragments of material from both the back and front seat and took those to the laboratory and prepared microscopic slides for examination and study."

"Doctor, without going into detail of each item found, did you find anything that was at all significant?"

"In the black Buick I examined stains, they were found to be rust stains. I examined from 30 to 40 different hairs from the floor and cushions and so forth and none of those hairs were any way similar to the hairs that I removed during the autopsy of Jo Ann Dewey. Nor, was there any evidence of human blood demonstrated in the vehicle. I even received the vacuumed material from the car."

"Doctor, don't testify about that," admonished the prosecutor, "I have laid no foundation for that whatsoever."

"All right."

"With reference to the items you personally took from the Pontiac and subsequently examined in the laboratory of the Oregon Medical School, did you make any findings that were significant?"

"None."

"Did you later examine the trunk of a Chevrolet coupe?"

"I examined this car at the Portland Police lot."

"When did you examine that car?"

"I may need to refer to my notes here," said the doctor as he leafed through a stack of papers in his lap, "I examined this car on the 18th of April, 1950."

"Did you personally recover from this car any items which you later examined in your laboratory?"

"Wait until I find my notes here on this, will you? Yes, now, I examined this car…"

"Will you first state what was recovered from the car?" interrupted Jones as he continued his rapid-fire line of prosecution.

"I received five items of dirt and hair from the back of the 1937 cream colored Chevrolet coupe."

"Tell what your findings were with reference to the examination of the hair sample, did you compare that hair with the known hair of Jo Ann Dewey?"

"I did."

"What were your findings, Doctor?"

"I found the hair of Jo Ann Dewey to be natural brown in color and I found this hair was brown in color, but it doesn't mean it was identical, only of the same similarity," reported the doctor.

"In connection with the comparison of hair from the human body, is there any positive way of identification with respect to hair, so far as comparison is concerned?"

"You cannot state it is identical but you can state a similarity in color and granules, but only a similarity. In other words, it is like green paint. We can identify green paint as being green, but we ordinarily remove hair from the head for microscopic study."

"Just proceed with the next item that was recovered."

"Well, the next hair, item 34-B, was a shaft about three-quarters of an inch in length and on its root end there was a red fleck of material where it was torn from the scalp."

"Did you find that hair was comparable with the known hairs of Jo Ann Dewey?"

"I can't state specifically but I can state it is of a natural, brown hair in color and there is a similarity. I can't state this is specifically her hair, it could be or could not be."

"In connection with the hair you have studied with respect to all the items that have been submitted to you, did you find at any other place that you have testified, hair which are similar in nature and comparable with Jo Ann Dewey's?"

"In the entire multitude of items I received there were only three hairs that had a similarity. All the rest of them were different in color and similarity."

"That is all," said Jones as Defense Attorney Goodman started his cross examination.

"What was your testimony with reference to blood in the black Buick, Doctor?" asked Goodman.

"We found no blood in that vehicle, what may look like blood to the average person, may be rust, and that is exactly what we found, rust particles."

"You found no blood at all in the automobile?"

"No blood at all."

"That is all, Doctor," ended Goodman's short cross exam.

The State had completed its testimony and was at rest. As soon as the pathologist left the courtroom so did the news reporters. They needed time to put together their stories of the day's events in court. The following day in bold, half-inch, black letters the front page headline read; "HAIR FOUND IN CAR MATCHES JO ANN'S".

CHAPTER TEN

"WILSON FAMILY TESTIMONIES"

As the Wilson family gathered in the "Waiting to Testify" area of the Vancouver courtroom, there were other happenings around the northwestern part of the United States. The swollen Columbia River had reached a level of almost nine feet above flood stage and was flowing hundreds of yards inland in and around the industrial areas of Vancouver, Washington shutting down manufacturing and compelling more than 100 men to take early vacations. During the month of June in 1950, some of those men went to court instead of work.

The trial got off to a slow start as the defense attorneys began the presentation of their case. The boy's mother, Eunice Wilson was on the stand that day when the issue of the missing power saw came up. Defense Attorney Goodman informed Judge Cushing that the issue of the missing power saw would come up many times in the course of the trial and asked to approach the bench. The judge agreed to hear some argument on the subject out of the presence of the jury.

While the jury was being escorted out of their seats Mrs. Wilson took the opportunity to lean forward in the stand and smile warmly at her sons sitting behind the defense table. After the last juror left the courtroom, all the attorneys approached the bench to hear the offer of proof from the defense regarding the illusive power saw.

"If Your Honor please," pleaded Goodman, "the defense wishes to make the following offer of proof with reference to the witness, Mrs. Eunice Wilson. If the witness were permitted to testify she would state that on Saturday, March 18th, 1950, she heard both her son's state that they intended to go to Silverton, Oregon on the following day to visit their father. That on the next day, she had a conversation with her sons wherein they told her that they were advised that a power saw had been stolen and that they were concerned about Utah's parole being revoked and that on the same night at 8:30 PM she was present with her sons when they stated that they would go to Portland for a few days and that the trip would be in the nature of a honeymoon for Utah and his wife. With the intent that if they stayed away for a few days the power saw matter might be cleared up and Utah's parole would not be violated because he had nothing to do with the theft of the power saw.

Mrs. Wilson would also testify that on or about Wednesday night of the same week, she had another conversation with her sons that they planned to go to California on account of the power saw situation because the police were looking for Utah and that they would be back from California by the time Utah was to report to his Parole Officer and that the alleged theft of the saw would then be cleared up and Utah exonerated of the charge."

The prosecutor objected to the offer of proof by the defense on the grounds that the testimony would be self-serving declarations on the part of the defendants and further that such conversations would be in the nature of hearsay evidence. The court sustained the objection whereupon the jury returned into court and questioning by the state appointed attorney, Sanford Clement continued. Mrs. Wilson was allowed limited testimony regarding the activities of her two sons. She started with the 18th of March when Turman had his teeth pulled at the dental clinic. Then when Clement asked her about any bruises on Turman's hands when she saw her son on the morning following Jo Ann's abduction, she stated she didn't see any cuts or bruises.

When asked about the money she was saving for Turman, she said she gave her son, "One thousand dollars in greenbacks."

On cross-examination, the prosecutor wanted Mrs. Wilson to retrace her son's activities.

"Mrs. Wilson, directing your attention to March 18th, which has been identified as a Saturday, you testified that Turman and Utah were together at your home on that date?

"That is right."

"When did they first leave your home on Saturday?"

"Let me just think a minute," the elderly woman paused but the prosecutor would only allow sharp quick answers.

It was a common law practice back in the 50's to try and get testimony entered into the trial so it could be considered as evidence if needed at a later date.

"How had Utah come to your home?" the prosecutor asked as he popped off his next question quickly.

"He came in the Pontiac, I believe."

"The boys owned a Pontiac, a Buick and a Chevrolet at that time?"

"Yes sir."

"Where was Utah living at that time?"

"Here in Vancouver."

"Had Utah stayed at your home on Friday night, March 17th?"

"No."

"Had Turman slept at your home on that occasion?"

"Yes sir."

"Utah came early Saturday morning of the 18th, how long was he there?"

"Well, he wasn't there very long until he went to the dentist. They left pretty early in the morning."

"When did you see them again?"

"In the afternoon at about seven o'clock. Turman went to bed shortly after he got home, he wasn't feeling good, he had two teeth pulled that day."

Unsatisfied that he couldn't make Eunice Wilson look like a befuddled old lady he dismissed her.

As she stepped off the witness stand and walked past her sons seated together with their lawyers the family resemblance was obvious especially in Utah who had his mother's slender sloped nose and high cheek bones while Turman got her high forehead gene.

Next Hazel Wilson, Grant's wife, whose occupation was identified as a housewife and mother was called to the stand and questioned first by the state appointed defense attorney, Sanford Clement. She was asked about riding in the cream colored, Chevrolet Coupe Turtleback. She testified that the family took the Chevrolet on picnics. That she had to put her head in the trunk several times to get stuff out. She also told the court that she often combed her short, brown hair in the car.

Under Jones' cross-examination, Hazel testified that two Vancouver policemen had come to her home looking for Turman. They were so intimidating she testified that they liked to have "scared the liver" out of her.

Immediately following his wife, Grant was put on the witness stand for a second time. Grant was a devout member of the Assembly of God church where he drove the church bus and taught a Sunday school class. Turman and Utah revered him as never having done a wrong thing in his life.

Upon direct examination the defense attorney tried to get admitted into evidence the stolen power saw in connection with the boy's reason for flight and the fact that Grant had witnessed someone removing beer bottles from Utah's garbage can but every answer by

Grant was followed by an objection from the prosecution which was followed by Judge Cushing sustaining it. After running out of questions for his witness the attorney returned to the defense table frustrated. Jones got up and started questioning Grant in a very different manner, not at all like the first time he was on the stand when he was called as a witness for the prosecution.

"What was Turman's trouble with the police on March 22nd?" asked Jones with a harsh voice.

"What was his trouble?" Grant asked, unclear of the prosecutor's question.

"Yes."

"The police were looking for him."

"When did any officer, to your personal knowledge, look for Turman?"

"I know they were looking for him all the time."

"I move the answer be stricken as not responsive," said Jones as he objected to the answer of his own question.

"Just tell me the date when the officers were looking for your brother, Turman."

"They never come to me personally. I know they didn't like him."

"You don't know that from your personal knowledge," snapped Jones.

"I know from my own knowledge how they treated him and were out to get him."

"I move the answer be stricken," declared Jones.

"The answer will be stricken from the record," said the judge.

"I am asking you, if you were ever with Turman when any police officer was looking for him, answer that yes or no," demanded Jones.

"Yes."

"When?"

"All the time."

"I move the answer be stricken," accosted Jones, as the verbal scuffle with Grant continued.

"Sustained," said the judge "and the answer is stricken, the jury will disregard it."

"I want the date, Grant and nothing more than that or less than that," lectured the prosecutor.

"It wasn't one day it was every day."

Abandoning this line of questioning before he lost his temper the prosecutor changed the line of questioning to the Pontiac.

"Now then, you say you abandoned this Pontiac on the streets of Portland and you were a party to that abandonment?"

"I parked the car and helped the boys take the clothes out and we left a coat and a full bottle of beer in the back seat of the car."

"That car was licensed in your name?"

"Yes."

"Why was it abandoned?"

"To turn the police away from Utah because it was about a power saw that had been stolen."

"Just a moment I move that be stricken and the jury directed to disregard it," objected Jones.

"The answer will be stricken and the jury is directed to disregard it," said the judge.

Not wanting any testimony about the power saw injected into the record the prosecuting attorney told the judge he was finished with Grant.

Judge Cushing looked at the clock on the wall of the courtroom and noticed it was a good time to break for lunch. He signaled to the bailiff to make the announcement.

"All rise!" announced the bailiff in a deep voice as the judge banged his gavel twice then stood and left the courtroom. Some reporters also left at this time to work on their stories and some spectators had to leave for unknown reasons but the majority of the spectators pulled out their sack lunches and began eating cold sandwiches so as to keep "dibs" on their seats. As the lunch break started drawing to a close, the sparse empty spaces on the hardwood benches in the courtroom started filling up once again.

During this interim an incident occurred over seating when an overweight woman had squeezed herself into a spot on the bench thereby crowding out a smaller woman. Incensed people who wanted justice for the smaller woman reported what they saw to Bailiff Al Cox. He shooed out all the people standing in the back of the room and then ejected the rude, heavy-set woman. The teeming courtroom applauded the bailiff's action. The woman was obviously embarrassed but forced a smile and performed a slight bow as she left.

The rest of the day's testimony was uneventful for the most part as Utah's mother-in-law; Gladys Cline was put on the witness stand and began her testimony to the packed courtroom. She was another witness for the defense who tried to testify about her son-in-law's fear of having his parole revoked because of the missing power saw but to no avail. Judge Cushing sustained every single objection the prosecutor made regarding Utah's fear of being arrested for the stolen power saw. There was no chance it was going to be admitted on record as evidence and the reason for leaving Washington State.

Next Utah agreed to waive his Fifth Amendment right by consenting to let his wife testify. Mrs. Lucille Wilson was a perky 17-year-old with short brown hair and sparkling eyes that were fresh and full of positive energy that made Utah feel like he was in another world every time he looked at her. She and Utah had been married less than a year when he was charged with first degree murder. She knew about his past because Utah confessed his criminal history to her before they were married. She was a strong youngster who knew in her heart he was not guilty of murder. Lucille stood with one hand on the Holy Bible and her other hand raised as the bailiff had her repeat the oath to tell the truth. She was told she could be seated as her husband's court appointed attorney started the questioning.

"Approximately what time did Utah get up on Sunday, March 19, 1950?"

"About 11:00."

"How was he dressed when he left the apartment that day?"

"He had blue slacks and a light tan, Twist sports jacket."

"What was Utah's general conduct and demeanor at the time he left?"

"Just as usual, happy, he went out the door singing."

"Later on that evening after Utah and Turman came back to your apartment. What was your destination when you three left the apartment together?"

"We went to Portland to the Morrison Hotel."

"Did you and Utah have a separate room from Turman?"

"Yes."

"What car did you drive at that time?"

"The Pontiac."

"How long did you stay at the Morrison Hotel?"

"Two nights."

"At any time was that referred to as a honeymoon?"

"Yes, the only one we got."

"How did you spend your time in Portland?"

"Going to shows."

"Was that the last time you saw your husband until he was returned to Vancouver?"

"Yes."

"How often do you see him?"

"Every time they would let me."

Asked if they kept bottled beer on hand she testified that they did once in a while, that Utah sometimes drank beer but very seldom. Upon inquiry as to whether Utah ever stood the empties on the curb she answered that he had lots of times and also that he tossed his empties from the car. She also stated that she had seen neighbor children remove the bottles from the curb.

On cross-exam the youthful witness was cautioned once during her testimony to "answer counsel's questions without smart remarks" after she replied in one instance that "she wasn't a walking dictionary."

The witness was excused whereupon Lucille Wilson got down from the witness stand and walked past the defense table giving her husband a sweet smile as he grinned back at her.

On Thursday, June 22, 1950, the state contended that the automobile used to take Jo Ann Dewey's body to the Wind River Canyon for dumping was the old 1937 Chevrolet. However, testimony of the morning witnesses, Dan McPherson, the purchaser of the Chevrolet and Edward Enright, the Wilson's personal mechanic both testified that the 1937 Chevrolet Coupe Turtleback the car the media dubbed as the "death car", was not moved from its parking place in front of Grant Wilson's home in Camas from March 17th to the day it was sold on March 28th. Mr. McPherson who purchased the car from the Wilson's testified it took him three days to get the car running. The witnesses told the jury that the battery on the car was dead, the generator was bad and that it had a flat tire. The state tried to prove this "death car" transported Jo Ann Dewey from Vancouver, sixty miles east to the Wind River in Carson, Washington.

The testimony regarding the condition of the car, where the car was parked and such continued until noon when the judge called for a recess. After the recess, Carl Whitney, a friend of Utah and Turman and witness for the defense was called into the courtroom to be questioned.

"Your name is Carl Whitney?" asked Defense Attorney Goodman after Carl had been sworn in and seated.

"Yes."

"Where do you live?"

"Kalama, Washington."

"How old are you?"

"Twenty-four."

"What kind of work do you do?"

To this question he identified himself as a power saw operator. A question by Goodman as to whether the witness knew that Utah was under parole brought a quick objection from the prosecutor who stated that this would be hearsay evidence.

"How did Whitney know this?" the prosecutor demanded.

Whitney answered that, "Utah had told him."

"This kind of testimony is not admissible," Jones declared, the records would have to be brought to court to prove it."

Goodman approached the subject in another way. He asked the witness if he was on parole and when he replied that he was Goodman shot back with a side glance at the prosecutor and said, "How do you know you're on parole Carl?"

"I spent five weeks in jail for it," the young man replied.

Attempts to get the power saw into the testimony were again blocked by Jones who objected to Goodman's questioning and was again sustained by Judge Cushing.

The witness testified that he had gone to the home of Gladys Cline and Lucille Cline-Wilson looking for Utah. He said he knew that Utah had worked at a logging operation on Larch Mountain cutting wood. A question to the witness as to what his purpose was in going to the Cline residence brought another objection from Jones. Goodman made an offer of proof and the jury filed out of their box.

The defense attorney pointed out that if Carl was allowed to testify that he was on parole and he hears that a power saw had been stolen and had gone to the Cline home to ask Utah if he knew anything about the theft that he would say that he feared his friends parole would be revoked and that he was also concerned about his own parole and wanted to learn the facts as both of them were innocent of the theft of the power saw.

Jones objected to the offer of proof on the grounds that the matter was not competent or relevant, that it would be strictly hearsay evidence and would constitute a self-serving declaration. His objections were sustained and the jury called back. On cross examination Carl said he had been convicted of first degree burglary in August with Utah Wilson.

After Carl left the stand a husky, widowed, farmwoman who rented part of her property to Mose Wilson testified. Her name was Stacie Goodman. She started her testimony off by stating that she was not related to the boy's attorney. She also said she saw the two boys on March 19th, when they came to her house in search of their father. She said the Wilson brothers were driving a black car, but she didn't know the make or model. She was a funny character who provided a lighter moment in court when she told Jones that she should be paid for her court appearance.

"I lost twelve dollars today by coming here," she said firmly, "I would have made that much picking berries at home."

Jones assured her she could collect her witness fees from the clerk's office. When she left the witness stand she declared that she wanted to shake hands with Mr. Goodman and the boys too. She carried out this action and sailed out of the courtroom. The dumbfounded attorneys shook themselves slightly and continued with the trial.

Next Goodman wanted to put Stacie's ten-year-old daughter Naoma Goodman on the stand. He knew he was taking a risk by putting her on the stand because children rarely ever make good witnesses. But she seemed mature for her age and with the back up testimony of her mother and older sister, he thought it was important to extensively establish that Turman and Utah were at their father's trailer in Silverton, Oregon just before nightfall on the night of Jo Ann's abduction.

Judge Cushing questioned the child first.

"State your name please."

"Naoma Goodman."

"How old are you?"

"Ten."

"Do you go to school?"

"Uh huh."

"What grade are you in?"

"Sixth."

"Do you know what it means to tell the truth?"

"Yes."

"Do you go to Sunday School?"

"No."

"Do you go to church?"

"I did when my daddy was alive but I don't anymore."

"When you went to church, they told you to tell the truth?"

"Yes."

"Will you tell the truth?"

"Yes."

"Go ahead Mr. Goodman," said the judge as he motioned in the direction of the defense table. The attorney stepped forward and started questioning the little girl.

"Will you tell the folks over in the jury box whether you know these two boys sitting over here? Can you see them from where you are sitting?"

"Yes," she answered.

"Are these the same boys sitting here in the courtroom, that you saw at your home on March 19th?"

"Yes."

"Were you playing baseball out in the street on Sunday, March 19th?"

"Yes."

"Was it getting pretty dark?"

"Yes."

"Did you see Turman and Utah Wilson after you had finished playing baseball?"

"I didn't see them."

"What?" he asked, taken aback by her unexpected answer.

"I didn't see them."

"You didn't see Turman and Utah Wilson in the evening?"

"No."

Perhaps the youngster misunderstood the question as her surprising answer backfired on the defense, made the prosecutor smirk and once again proved that children are high risk witnesses.

CHAPTER ELEVEN

"TURMAN TAKES THE STAND"

It was another packed courtroom at 1200 Franklin Street in Vancouver, Washington. This new day of testimony brought Turman Wilson to take the stand on his own behalf.

Turman was wearing a tan, tweed coat over grayish blue pants with a tan, striped shirt and tie. His brown hair was slicked back off his high forehead as he walked with confidence to the witness stand. The bailiff asked him to raise his right hand and put his left hand on the Bible.

The bailiff then asked him, "Do you swear to tell the truth the whole truth and nothing but the truth, so help you God?"

"I do," replied Turman.

"You may be seated," directed the bailiff as he returned to his designated post, while Goodman walked toward his client.

"Turman, you are one of the defendants in this case?'

"Yes, I am."

"Turman, I want to go back a little ways, since your release from the Oregon Penitentiary, have you been arrested on several occasions?"

"Yes."

"Tell the jury about that in your own words."

Turman proceeded to tell numerous stories of his misadventures with the Vancouver Police. He was put in a lot of line ups and never identified as a perpetrator. He was accused of stealing a car that was lent to him by his brother. He told of occasions when he was told to stay out of town and was threatened many times by local authorities. Turman carried on for about 45 minutes when the prosecutor shouted, "I object!"

"Sustain the objection."

"Can you name the dates and places?" asked his attorney.

"Different times during the day and evening."

"Can you name some of the officers involved?"

"Yes."

"Go ahead."

"Bob Lord on two or three occasions in Vancouver and Officer Borgan told me to stay out of town and told me not to be seen in town or my legs would be shot out from under me. Sometimes I was stopped and I didn't even know the policeman who stopped me but they had the license number of the Chevrolet I was driving but it was registered in Grant's name and at the time I was arrested at Washougal in Grant's house the car was in Grant's name and Bob Lord was going to confiscate my car…"

"I object, this witness should state the facts."

The objection was sustained by the court.

"Do you recall the occasion when some 14 police officers came out to get you?" asked Goodman.

"That was the occasion I referred to at Grant's home. They previously had been sitting in the vicinity of my mother's house. I knew the police were after me for something because I had seen them at mother's house."

"I object and move that be stricken," interrupted the prosecutor.

"Sustain the objection and the answer will be stricken and the jury directed to disregard it" instructed the judge.

"On all of these occasions you have been arrested and investigated, were all of the charges against you dismissed?" continued the defense attorney.

"Yes, except of the charge I was acquitted on."

"Do you know Officer Ulmer?"

"Yes I do."

"When did you first meet Officer Ulmer?"

"In Sacramento, California."

"Had Officer Ulmer threatened you?

"Yes, he told me that he had heard many things about me and he was going to see to it that I had my neck stretched and he said if I did happen to get out of these charges facing me now there were many things in Vancouver that I would be charged with."

"Did Officer Ulmer tell you on or about April 1, 1950, what would happen to you when Sheriff

Anderson and the other Vancouver officers arrived in Sacramento?"

"He told me that if I didn't confess to him and Borgan that when he got through with me Sheriff Anderson wouldn't recognize me."

"Turman, what explanation do you give to the jury for not having notified the mill yourself that you were taking a leave?"

"Well, I was out there by the Lacamas Lake and at that time I hadn't intended going into town and I asked Grant would he notify the mill because he would be near a phone and I wanted the mill to be notified before 4:00 PM and I wanted them to have plenty of time to get somebody to work in my place and I asked Grant to tell them I wouldn't be there until the following Thursday at which time I had planned to be back at work."

"Why did you not have a car in your name?"

"Usually I was chased around by the police…"

"I object," interjected Jones, "if he wants to state the dates and places I have no objection but I object to his drawing his own conclusions that is for the jury."

"Sustained."

"Turman, can you tell the jury what the mechanical condition of the Buick was as of March 17th?"

"Yes it needed a few repairs. I took it to a garage and he spent four or five minutes checking it and the clutch was nearly gone and he advised the clutch might play out in a week or two and advised that I should have it fixed and he also looked at the carburetor and told me it needed new spark plugs and he did something to the clutch and it worked a little better but it wasn't too good."

Turman had been on the witness stand all day when one of the jurors suddenly fell ill around 3:00 PM. The juror asked the judge to call for a recess while he rested for about a half hour. When he still didn't feel well he was discharged from duty. However it was too late to continue questioning Turman so court was adjourned.

On the following day the replacement juror was drawn at random from the two alternate jurists and took seat number seven in the jury box. Turman's lengthy dissertation was replaced by Q&A with his own lawyer. After the routine courtroom procedures his testimony began with the visit to the Playhouse Theatre in Portland, Oregon.

"After you and Utah left the Jolly Joan Restaurant, what did you do?" asked Goodman.

"We went to a theatre in Portland."

"What theatre?"

"The Playhouse."

"Did you ever attend the Playhouse Theatre any other night or any other time during the month of March, 1950?"

"No I didn't but previously I had attended it many times."

"You had worked the night shift at the Washougal Woolen Mill a great deal during that period of time?"

"Yes all the time except Saturdays and Sundays."

"So you didn't have any nights of the week off isn't that so?"

"That is correct."

"So that there will be no misunderstanding on this point, is it your testimony to this jury that the only time during the month of March that you attended the Playhouse Theatre was Sunday, March 19, 1950?"

"That's right."

"How long did you stay at the Playhouse Theatre?"

"We left the Playhouse Theatre I would say about 12:15, the final show was concluded and we walked up to where the car was parked two blocks away and the parking meters were all used up when we parked our car and after we…"

"Turman, what time was the show over?"

"About 12:10 I would say."

"Utah was with you all of that time?"

"Yes."

Shortly before noon Goodman finished questioning Turman. Then Jones began the cross-examination that covered the defendant's life for the past eight years.

"Mr. Wilson, in the opening part of your direct examination you had advised the court that the first felony for which you were convicted was the crime of forcible rape?"

"Rape, yes."

"That was forcible rape?'

"It was a charge of rape which I plead guilty to."

"Would you care to state the details in connection with that crime?"

"Your honor," objected Goodman "I am going to make very few objections but I am going to object to this question because that would be trying another case over in the trial of this case."

"He can answer yes or no," stated the judge.

"Do you care to tell the circumstances in connection with the first felony conviction?"

"No."

"Would you care to state whether others were involved with you or not?"

"No."

"You do not care to state?"

"No."

"You do not care to give any detail at all about that matter?"

"Well I have done time for it and I paid very dearly for that offense."

"At that time you were 16 years old?"

"Yes."

"When you took your employment in October of 1949 at the Washougal Woolen Mill you had no money saved up?"

"None, I had money upon my release from the Oregon Penitentiary, I had several hundred dollars."

"Where had you obtained that?"

That was obtained more or less under an agreement or a little business I guess I don't believe I will state to the court."

"You don't care to relate how you got the money, can you tell how much you had with you at that time?"

"Does it matter how much money I had?"

"It would probably not be material but we introduced the money taken from you upon your apprehension in Sacramento. From then on it develops your thrift and frugality and I'm interested in following it up. If you claim privilege of the source I would like to know the amount?"

"If it becomes necessary I can prove $1,400."

"So you had $1,400 when you took employment at the Washougal Woolen Mills?"

"I had previously spent some money on my release from the Oregon Penitentiary I had $1,400."

"You mean you had $1,400 when you went into the Oregon State Penitentiary?"

"I had $1,400 upon my release."

"You don't want to state how you acquired it?"

"I don't believe it is necessary to state how I acquired the money."

"You have made various statements about the officers and their conduct. Have you ever suffered any physical injury at the hands of any of them?"

"They have never touched me, no."

"Didn't you in connection with your return from California state that you received excellent treatment?"

"On my return trip I did receive good treatment. However before that time I had not received good treatment."

"What treatment did you receive and by what persons who didn't treat you good?"

"At the time I was put in jail at Sacramento I tried to contact an attorney but I was told by three different fellows that orders had been received from Vancouver, Washington that I was to receive no counsel and upon the arrival of Borgan and Ulmer they threatened me several times."

"Did either Borgan or Ulmer ever put hands on you?"

"No."

The prosecutor questioned Turman extensively over the activities of him and his brother from March 18th through the end of the month, Jones even called for a blackboard in order for the witness to make a drawing of the roads he and his brother had traveled during that time frame.

"Why did you use the name of Ted E. Davis?"

"Because if they tried to trace Utah they would trace him through relatives."

"So you were using false and fraudulent names?"

"I wasn't frauding any names I was using alias names. I always used them except on business or employment."

"We have no further questions at this time," concluded Jones as he turned his back on Turman and returned to his seat.

"Your honor please I have just a few more questions," said Goodman as he approached his client, "Turman you have been on the witness stand quite a long time and I want to ask you just a few questions. I understand you waived extradition and voluntarily returned to Vancouver?"

"Yes I did."

"When you were arrested in Sacramento by the FBI you gave your true name?"

"I did."

"You also gave them your correct address?"

"Yes."

"That is all."

Turman Wilson was on the witness stand a total of eight hours when he stepped down from the stand he appeared unruffled. His only sign of weariness during his entire testimony was the constant blinking of his dark brown eyes as the hours wore on.

CHAPTER TWELVE

"UTAH TAKES THE STAND"

Utah Eugene Wilson turned twenty years old in 1950; he was the youngest of the six Wilson boys born to Eunice and Mose Wilson. He talked very little but friends and family described him as a happy-go-lucky kid. He had a round face and elfish grin that made everyone comfortable around him. He ended his education in the public school system while in the ninth grade. Teachers passed him through grades never finding out he couldn't read. His big brother Turman was his constant companion.

On the witness stand Utah appeared weary after the long hours in court. He had lost weight, his face was thin and it showed signs of stress and strain. Like his brother he shared the same details of his activities. He explained being at the Dental Clinic with his brother, then going to Silverton to visit their father, watching the two "Captain" movies at the Playhouse Theatre that lasted until after midnight and spending the misty morning at Lacamas Lake roasting hotdogs over a small fire with Turman. His attorney then questioned him regarding what he did on Tuesday, March 21st the day after the abduction.

"In a sentence or two, can you tell the jury what you did on that day?"

"Well, I believe we slept late that morning and just got down and parked the Pontiac in a parking lot and were just walking around the corner and my wife and Turman and I were going to the Circle Theatre in Portland."

"Let's come to Wednesday, March 22nd, Utah did you meet anybody in Portland on that day?"

"My mother-in-law, my wife and Turman and I met them."

"It was a surprise?"

"Yes."

"You were making Monday and Tuesday a sort of honeymoon?"

"Yes we figured as long as we were going to be out of Vancouver a couple of days or a little longer."

"Were you dressed the same on Wednesday as you were on Monday and Tuesday?"

"Yes we were."

"And on the Sunday preceding?"

"Yes."

"Why did you go to Medford, Oregon?"

"We wanted to get me a job so I had asked my Probation Officer, Mr. O'Brien on different occasions if it would be possible to get a job out of the state. I was on probation or parole, one way or another and he told me the only way that would be possible would be to have a job and I figured if I could get a job and come back and tell my probation officer I had a job he would fix it so I could leave Vancouver and get out of the State of Washington."

"Did you find work in Medford?"

"No."

"When you were arrested in Sacramento did you give the officers your true name?"

"Yes, I did."

"Without mentioning any names, did any officer swear at you on the way back from Sacramento?"

"On the way back when we stopped at one restaurant."

"Did they swear at you in Sacramento?"

"Yes they did."

"Utah, I have two more questions. You are charged by Mr. Jones, as Prosecuting Attorney with two crimes, the first being murder in the first degree and the second being kidnapping in the first degree both of the crimes involved the kidnapping and death of Jo Ann Dewey. Did you ever know or had you ever seen Jo Ann Dewey in her lifetime?"

"I hadn't."

"Had you ever heard the name of Jo Ann Dewey until after Sunday, March 19, 1950?"

"No I didn't."

"You may cross-examine," said Goodman.

It was around 11:30 in the morning when Jones started his questioning. His cross-examination was as intense as had been the older brother's the day before. He pounded relentlessly where any hesitancy was apparent in Utah's answers. Jones tried to compel the defendant to recount every hour of his life spent in the area before he left for California.

Jones skipped around a lot with his questions. He would drop one subject to lead the defendant onto another topic before returning to pursue the former theme. In an explanation as to why they had abandoned the Pontiac, Utah tried to explain, but was told by Jones to stick to the questions that were being asked.

"Did you go to Camas before you went into Portland?"

"That is sort of hard to say I couldn't say for sure," Utah answered.

"Why is it so hard to remember?"

"There are so many dates here it is too hard to keep going."

"You told about your activities on the 19th?"

"Yes."

"Why are you more certain about the 19th than other dates?" "Because I am charged with murder that's why," responded Utah with a raised voice.

"I have a few more questions regarding your probation. After you plead guilty to some burglaries did this court put you on probation?"

"That's right."

"They gave you a deferred sentence?"

"That's right."

"That was done by Judge Cushing?"

"That's right."

"You understood that was the only person that could revoke that parole was the Judge of the Superior Court?"

"I didn't know it, no."

"You mean your Probation Officer, Mr. Frank O'Brien didn't explain that to you?"

"No one explained anything."

"Mr. O'Brien started your probation in November of 1949?"

"September, I believe it was."

"September of 1949?"

"That's right."

"Do you remember when you made your first report to Mr. O'Brien?"

"I believe that was in November."

"Your treatment from Mr. O'Brien has been good?"

"Very good, yes."

"When was your last conference with him?"

"It was a couple of months before I was placed in jail here."

"At that time he talked to you about your probation in general?"

"Yes."

"And in getting a job?"

"Yes."

"And he also talked to you about running around with your brother, Turman?"

"I think Turman might have been mentioned."

"Isn't it a fact that on March 16, 1950 at your home in Vancouver, he told you that you could not run around with Turman and told you not to be in his company?"

"No."

"And you said to Mr. O'Brien that your brother sometimes comes to visit you and he told you that would be all right but you were not to be out with Turman?"

"He never even told me to stay away from Turman."

"Were there any other things he talked about in connection with your probation?"

"He talked about a couple of things, it was on three or four different occasions, I don't remember the date. I talked to him and I asked him if it would be possible for me to leave the state and he told me it wouldn't without I had a job waiting for me where I went, and he told me he would try to get a job for me out of Vancouver but he didn't say much about out of the state."

"In any event you saw your Probation Officer and had some talk with him on the night of March 16, 1950?"

"Around there yes."

"You didn't attempt to get in touch with Mr. O'Brien after March 19, 1950?"

"No I didn't."

"You didn't attempt to contact Judge Cushing in connection with this deferred sentence?"

"I didn't."

"You didn't come to the Prosecuting Attorney in connection with that matter?"

"I didn't."

"You didn't go to the Sheriff's office here to talk to some friends that were interested in your welfare?"

"I didn't."

"You did go to the Sheriff's office on March 19th didn't you?"

"Somewhere around there."

"Do you remember going to the Sheriff's office one evening to take some fish you caught?"

"Yes, I do."

"Who were you going to see on that occasion?"

"I was going to see Mr. Luce but he wasn't in so I gave them to Markley."

"Didn't you tell Mr. Markley you caught that fish at Bonneville Dam in Skamania County?"

"I didn't tell him that, I told him it was on the Columbia River."

"Didn't you tell Mr. Markley you had been fishing on the White Salmon River?"

"I believe not and if you will get him in here he will say the same thing."

"Did you see Mr. O'Brien after you were in custody and were in the Clark County Jail?"

"Yes I did."

"Do you remember when that was?"

"After I was picked up at Sacramento and was awaiting trial in jail."

"Didn't you tell him that there wasn't anything in connection with the probation that caused you to leave Vancouver?"

"No that's the reason I left."

"What did you tell him?"

"The exact words I told Mr. O'Brien when I left Washington I did not think I was breaking my parole just to be leaving but I knew if I was staying or moving without his permission I would be breaking it.

"I don't quite follow?"

"I will make it a little simpler. He knows if I go over to Portland that is over in Oregon. I wouldn't break my parole but if I went to Portland to live I would be breaking my parole."

"Did you receive the rules in connection with your probation?"

"I didn't receive anything."

"Mr. O'Brien didn't give you any?"

"Nothing, he didn't give me nothing."

"That is all," said Jones after Utah had been on the stand for a total of 2 1/2 hours.

"I have a few questions on redirect examination, your honor," said Goodman as he walked towards his client.

"Was there any restriction on your associating with your own brother?"

"I was never told it, no."

"Your brother is not on probation or parole?"

"No."

"You are fond of Turman aren't you?"

"Very fond of him."

"That is all."

CHAPTER THIRTEEN

"THE USHERETTE CONTROVERSY"

The tug of war began bright and early first thing Monday morning, June 26, 1950 in Judge Cushing's courtroom as the defense team exploded a bombshell in the Wilson murder trial. Betty Mae Lyon, an 18-year-old with curly, blonde hair, who stood 5' 1" tall strolled into Judge Cushing's courtroom with an air of confidence. She looked stunning in her crisp freshly dry cleaned gray suit, wearing a pink hat with blue trim. She also had a plastic black purse hanging neatly off her left shoulder.

The anticipation from the audience caused an electricity in the air that was palpable as the attractive blonde was sworn in to testify. Sanford Clement was well prepared as he approached the vibrant teenager and started the questioning.

"Did you ever work at the Playhouse Theatre in Portland, Oregon?" asked Clement.

"Yes."

"How long did you work at the Playhouse Theatre?"

"One day only."

"Do you remember what night that was definitely?"

"Sunday, March 19, 1950."

"Mrs. Lyon, do you recall having a conversation with two young men in the lobby of the Playhouse Theatre on Sunday, March 19, 1950?"

"Yes I do."

"Will you point out the two young men?"

"Yes."

"Your honor, I would like to have the record show she pointed to Utah Wilson and Turman Wilson."

"The record may show," acknowledged Judge Cushing.

"Do you recognize Mr. Jones, the Prosecuting Attorney?"

"Yes I do."

"Did Mr. Jones at any time interview you?"

"Yes."

"When was that?"

"Friday."

"Did anybody try to confuse you as to the date you worked at the Playhouse Theatre?"

Jones jumped up from his chair like it was on fire, "That question is highly improper and I object."

"Sustained."

"Betty," continued the state appointed defense attorney, "did anybody in your interview attempt to tell you that you worked in the Playhouse Theatre on Monday, March 20th instead of March 19th?"

"I object to that as an improper question!" exclaimed Jones as he jumped to his feet again.

"Sustain the objection," ruled the judge again.

"I have one more question I would like to get out before the prosecutor jumps up again," said Clement.

"Go ahead," acquiesced the judge.

"Has anybody threatened you in respect to your testimony in this case?"

"That's why I had to be picked up and brought over here today."

Betty was calm, cool and collected on the witness stand and went on to testify that she had told Jones during their interview that if she could see the two young men in person she was convinced she would recognize them. She added that she had glanced at the younger brother two or three times in the lobby of the theater as he approached her because he looked familiar. She said she would be able to recognize Turman by his voice, declaring that she never forgets a voice.

Following the surprising testimony of Betty were three other usherettes working that night. Mrs. Arlene Griffith, 22, of Portland Oregon, Miss Mary Rustebakke, 19, also from Portland who no longer worked at the theater but was employed at the Jantzen knitting mills, and Betty Stephens, 18, of Tacoma, Washington, all three former usherettes testified to working with Betty that evening.

The attorneys next came to superfluous blows in the courtroom when Cleo Wilson, the soft spoken head usherette and fifth woman working in the theatre on Sunday night was put on the stand. It was pointed out to the jury that Mrs. Wilson was not related to Utah, Turman or any of the Wilson clan that had come from the Midwest. The comely brunette who provided a touch of glamour to the courtroom scene was questioned and cross-examined for an hour and 45 minutes. She recalled that the boys came to the theater where she was working behind the refreshment bar between the hours of 8:30 PM and 9:00 PM in March. She produced her hand written records of the usherette's schedule and the war began over getting it admitted into the trial as official evidence.

"When did you first contact Betty Lyon?" asked Goodman, as he took over the questioning for the defense team.

"Soon after you came to me and asked me about this. I contacted all of the girls that worked on March 19th and asked them if they recalled the conversation I had with the two boys."

"Did you have an official record you made up in connection with the Playhouse Theatre's payroll?"

"Yes, I had a time book that I turned in to the assistant manager."

"I have in my hand Defendant's Exhibit number 65," said the boy's attorney as he waved around a small loose leaf notebook for everyone in the courtroom to see "is this time book a part of your official record as head usherette at the Playhouse Theatre?"

The prosecutor leaped out of his chair, "it wouldn't be a part of the OFFICIAL record," objected Jones.

Undaunted by Jones interruption, Goodman continued his line of questioning regarding the time book, "Is it a part of your record in your capacity as head usherette?"

"Yes sir."

"I wish you would look at the exhibit and tell the jury if it is in your own handwriting?"

"It has some of my handwriting and some of the assistant manager's too."

"Your witness," said Goodman as he returned the book to the evidence table before sitting down.

"Mrs. Wilson, where has this been?" asked Jones as he picked up the book.

"At the theatre."

"Whereabouts at the theatre?"

"The candy bar."

"When did you obtain it?"

"Last night, I went into the theatre about 8:00 PM."

"Who was with you?"

"Mr. Bacon."

"Who is Mr. Bacon?"

"He is the assistant manager of the Liberty Theatre in Camas."

"Where did you meet Mr. Bacon?"

"At Eleventh and Morrison, he was on the corner and as I went back to the car he engaged me in conversation and said he was there to get the payroll book for Mr. Jones."

"That is very odd, because I've never heard of Mr. Bacon, did he have the keys to the theatre with him?"

"Yes sir."

"In his pocket?" quizzed Jones.

"I imagine," responded Cleo firmly.

"Do you know his first name?"

"Frank."

"What exactly is his occupation?"

"He is the assistant manager of the Liberty Theatre in Camas."

"If the court please," said Jones as he held up Cleo's time book, "we object to the introduction of exhibit number 65, it is nothing more than a memorandum."

"Before Your Honor rules on that," said Goodman as he approached the judge's platform, "I want to interrogate the witness further."

"Go ahead," said the judge.

"Referring to the week ending March 27th, will you find that page again?"

"It is the first page in the book. We previously had sheets we filled out and we ran out of sheets so I started this book."

"Does that page show what hours Betty Lyon worked?"

"It shows she worked four hours the previous week."

"Objection!" interjected Jones, "until the person in charge can identify it as an official record it would not be admissible in connection with the hours worked of any employee."

"May I be heard?" Goodman asked the judge.

"Yes sir," said Judge Cushing.

"Your honor please," implored Goodman, "this time book is a part of Cleo Wilson's record as head usherette."

Do you maintain this is an official record of the Company?" asked the judge.

"Yes," said Goodman.

"It is only a memorandum," maintained Jones as he interrupted the conversation between Goodman and Judge Cushing.

"I will sustain the objection until it is properly identified," ruled the judge.

"May I explain why I hadn't…" asked Cleo, shaking and on the verge of tears when the prosecutor interrupted her and took control of the scene.

He severely admonished the head usherette, "This witness isn't to explain anything until she is asked and I object to the volunteer statement."

"Sustain the objection," ruled the judge, "just answer the questions."

"Do you know whether Betty Lyon received any pay for any work at the Playhouse Theatre other than for March 19, 1950?" continued the defense.

"No, she…"

"I object to that!" snapped Jones, "This witness is not competent to testify."

"Sustain the objection," ruled the judge as he once again sided with the prosecution. Cleo couldn't take the harsh treatment. Her eyes welled up with tears that flowed down her cheeks and she was dismissed from the witness stand.

The defense fought hard to prove that Betty Lyon was paid for working on the 19th of March but in the end the judge sided with the prosecution that the official time record to be admitted into evidence was the record kept by the manager and not Cleo's handwritten sheets of paper. Even though numerous eyewitnesses working on that Sunday, the busiest night of the week, testified that Betty Mae Lyon was working at the Playhouse Theatre in Portland, Oregon. The only evidence Judge Cushing would allow into the trial's transcript were records that did NOT show Betty working that evening. This was a knockdown blow to the defense team but Turman and Utah still had high hopes of being judged fairly by the jury.

Years later during the appeals process more theater drama was resurrected into the lime light when a "Motion for New Trial" was filed on the grounds of newly discovered evidence for the defendants. A Miss Eva Adams stated in an affidavit that Turman and Utah Wilson sat next to her in the Playhouse Theatre on March 19, 1950 and that they were there from 9:00 PM until after midnight. Eva had contacted Goodman's law office and spoke to one of his colleagues about three days before the Wilson case went to the jury. She stated that for business and personal reasons she couldn't possibly become involved, have her name

publicly mentioned or involve the gentleman who
accompanied her to the theater that night without first
getting his consent. Unfortunately the defense team
was unable to produce the information from Eva until
after the jury had rendered its verdict and the final
curtain came down on the Usherette Controversy at the
Playhouse Theatre.

CHAPTER FOURTEEN

"CLOSING THE CASE"

Wednesday, June 28, 1950, as had been the routine for the past two weeks the Wilson brothers were brought from their fifth-floor jail cell in the county courthouse to Judge Cushing's courtroom. Deputies escorted them down the hall and into the courtroom, through the judge's chambers. Just before they entered the courtroom their handcuffs and shackles were removed and they were taken to their seats next to their two attorneys. This was the day for closing arguments. The attorney for the prosecution went first. He spent an hour and ten minutes presenting his closing arguments. He emphasized the beer bottle found by police officers at the scene of the abduction and stated as follows:

"Fingerprints found on the beer bottle of Utah Wilson are one of the most positive pieces of identification there is. This is one calling card that God has equipped each individual with that no one in this world can duplicate. The defense would like to have you believe that beer bottles were carelessly tossed all over town but only one!" Jones emphasized as he shot his right index finger straight up over his head, "was found at the scene of the crime. Utah Wilson was driving around that night and he was the one who threw out that bottle and that's the bottle that was found in the street by the Vancouver police.

What would be more natural than for the younger of the two, who was probably less schooled in criminal procedure to bolster up his courage by drinking a bottle of beer?" Jones rhetorically asked the jury as he continued his summation, "The activity of the two brothers alone declares them guilty," said Jones as he systematically retraced the steps of Turman and Utah after the abduction of Jo Ann Dewey.

Then like a butcher carving a piece of meat, the skilled prosecutor tore into Grant Wilson's personal character regardless of the fact that Grant was a witness for the prosecution and had no criminal history. Jones went on to berate Grant for his nervousness throughout the whole trial.

"I don't blame anyone related to the Wilson brothers for taking the stand and trying to help one of his own but I condemn Grant Wilson because of the knowledge he had that his brothers had abducted Jo Ann Dewey."

Changing the subject Jones scanned the faces of the men and women in the jury box as he continued, "I'd like to remind you ladies and gentlemen of the jury that Jo Ann's hairs were found in the 1937 Chevrolet Coupe Turtleback. Even though hair is not a positive form of identification the hairs found were similar in pigment, granulation and texture of Jo Ann's and this testimony was presented to you by Dr. Richardson who happens to be one of the most experienced men in pathology."

Next Jones refreshed the memory of the jury by reciting the testimony of a resident from the Central Court Apartments.

"Mrs. Nelson was an eye-witness to Jo Ann being brutally beaten. After Mrs. Nelson saw the pictures of the defendants in the newspapers she came to the jail where she picked them out of a line up. She has clearly identified Turman, as being one of the girl's abductors. She witnessed a man wearing a gray suit on that night, being of medium build and having dark, slicked-back hair. I say to you good people of the jury that Turman Wilson has dark, slicked-back hair is of medium build and, "pointing his finger towards the defense table Jones glared at Turman then announced, "he came to court wearing a gray suit at one time during this trial."

Jones scoffed at the testimony of the usherettes with a disdainful attitude as he continued his closing argument.

"Even if Betty Mae Lyon was at the Playhouse Theatre on March 19th at 9:00 in the evening this still would not be an alibi but only more testimony. The State of Washington is so fortunate in having obtained so much proof of guilt in this case. Even though this case has been a long one and we have all come to know each other by the tragic event of a young girl's death, this case is not about personalities it's the proof of how we are going to be governed in the future."

Jones concluded his lengthy dissertation then returned to his seat.   Goodman knew he was next to present his closing argument to the jury and rose to his feet before the prosecutor sat down.   Speaking in a low, even voice Goodman began a four hour long discourse. He started with reasonable doubt. He stated that the state had no foundation whatsoever for a case.

"You eight men and four women sitting here today must be convinced beyond a shadow of a doubt that the crime was committed between the hours of 11:00 PM and midnight on March 19, 1950," he stated.

Then he began an analysis of the testimony of all the witnesses who took the stand for the state declaring that not one could identify the kidnappers.

"Mrs. Nelson is a confused woman. It was three weeks after Jo Ann had been abducted when Mrs. Nelson was taken to the Clark County jail. Then with the assistance of Police Chief Harry Diamond she identified Turman and Utah as the assailants. Mrs. Nelson's description of the two men on Sunday night consists of a man with dark hair and another man larger than the first. That's it! By her own testimony she says that she had gone to bed and was reading the newspaper when she heard the screams and that she had risen to her knees to peer out the window. This means that a bedroom light had to be on when she was looking out the window. There was no evidence that the light was ever turned off. Therefore Mrs. Nelson was looking from a distance in a lighted room into the darkness to see those men," he said with an incredulous expression on his face. After pausing long enough to allow the jury to ponder the difficulty involved when peering into the darkness from a lighted room Goodman continued.

"You couldn't get any other apartment resident to swear to that kind of testimony. In fact Mr. Andrews who lives in the same apartment building as Mrs. Nelson testified that after hearing screams of terror, when he couldn't see anything from his own apartment window, rushed to the street below and that's when he saw one man walking toward a vehicle and only the top of the head of another person inside the car. Mr. Andrews was outdoors at the time of the abduction and not in a lighted room looking through a glass window. No other Central Court Apartment witness was able to pick Turman or Utah out of a line up," said Goodman shaking his head in a gesture of disbelief.

As he paced back and forth in front of the jury box he continued, "Now this brings us up to the alleged death car. You heard the prosecutor himself say and I quote, 'that officers didn't get busy about this car until late in the case' but I would like to remind you that the so called "death car" had a dead battery, a flat tire and sat parked on the street in front of Grant Wilson's home in Camas. You have heard multiple witnesses testify to the fact that the car was never moved between March 17th and the end of the month when it had to be towed away.

The prosecuting attorney would like you to think that hair samples found in the trunk of the Wilson family car are admissible evidence in this case in fact they are not. You have also heard that although the hairs found in the car are similar, I repeat similar to those of Jo Ann's all the women in the Wilson family also have short brown hair and have ridden in the Chevrolet Coupe Turtleback many times. The four hairs out of a whole host of hair samples taken form the car by the pathologist prove nothing."

Goodman declared that he was not accusing any of the State's witnesses of telling untruths as he continued to address the jury, "I don't believe and I don't think you believe the statements of Detectives Borgan and Ulmer and yet they were very, very deep in the case. I believe the men who truly destroyed the life of Jo Ann Dewey will be apprehended and removed from society and that some day the truth in this case will come out." After four hours the defense attorney had finished his closing argument. Next the clerk handed the jury instructions dictated earlier by Judge Cushing. All 12 of them read along as the judge dictated his instructions.

"It becomes my duty as judge," said Cushing, "to instruct you in the law that applies in this case and it is your duty as jurors to follow the law as I shall state it to you. It is the law of the land that a person is presumed to be innocent until overcome by proof of guilt beyond a reasonable doubt."

The judge defined reasonable doubt to the jury along with willful felony, rape, larceny, robbery and murder in the first degree. He also made sure the jurors were crystal clear on the fact that when two people are involved in committing the same crime they are equally guilty to the same degree as though they had individually committed the crime.

Halfway through the instructions he told the jury that "circumstantial evidence is entitled to the same weight as direct evidence. Strong circumstantial evidence is often the most satisfactory of any from which to draw the conclusion of guilt. If you find from the evidence that the defendants have previously been convicted of a crime this is not of itself evidence of guilt in this case but it is a circumstance to be weighed and considered in the determination of the weight or credibility that you should give to their testimony."

The judge also gave the jury instructions regarding Turman and Utah's alibi.

"You are instructed that the defense of an alibi to be entitled to consideration must be such as to show that at the very time of the commission of the crime the accused were at another place so far away or under such circumstances that they could not, with an ordinary exertion have been at that place where the alleged crime was committed. If you believe from the evidence that the accused were not so far away from the place where the crime was committed but that they could with ordinary exertion have reached the place where the offense was committed then you will consider that fact as a circumstance tending to prove or disprove the alibi."

The jury was instructed not to consider any of the opening statements or closing arguments of the attorneys.

"You should bring to bear a judgment that is cool, calculating, deliberate and fearless," emphasized the judge.

Finally the jury was told to select someone to act as foreman to preside over the deliberations and to sign the verdicts.   The jury of Turman and Utah's "peers" that retired to deliberate their fate consisted of four women and eight men all over the age of 35. Two weeks prior 58 prospective lay people were called for jury duty. Thirteen of them were excused for cause immediately and others were excused upon their own requests because they had already formed fixed opinions as to the guilt of the defendants and could not act impartially in the case because of newspaper articles. At that time potential jurors were interrogated as to their personal and religious feelings on the death penalty or whether they had personal ideas in conflict with the kidnapping law. One was disqualified because they opposed the death penalty. The defense asked the small group in the jury panel if they would give the brothers the benefit of the doubt if the evidence brought out showed that the pair had been convicted of previous crimes, could they return a fair verdict without taking this into consideration? The questioning droned on for almost three full days until finally the jury panel was exhausted and a substantial and mature group was accepted.   All were married and nine of the 12 jurors had children. The four women members of the jury were housewives. The men were retired farmers, others were clerks, two were employed at the woolen mills, there was a school principal and another was an employee of the PUD. At the start of the trial they were sworn in and remained together at all times. This was the group who exited the courtroom and went down the hall to a small anteroom that had been set up for their arrival. Paper, pencils and thick, glass ashtrays were neatly arranged down the center of a long table which was flanked by six chairs on each side.

While the jury deliberated, Turman and Utah were routinely escorted like any other day of the past two weeks of the trial back to their jail cells.

Turman stood in the open doorway of the gray bars that kept him confined as the deputy removed his handcuffs. As the cold, steel bars slammed shut behind him he trudged silently over to his metal cot. He flopped backwards onto the wool blanket that was spread over a thin, lumpy mattress and laid his head down on a small jail issued pillow. Lying there staring at the cement block ceiling, thoughts of the past few months started to float around in his mind like hand-painted scenes on a carousel circling around in his head. He knew he wasn't a model citizen of society but he was absolutely innocent of murder. He was sure the jury had to see the events that took place in the month of March played out as clearly and as innocently as he was seeing it now.

It had been a grueling and at times an exciting trial but the moment Turman had waited for had come. He got to tell his side of the story. A peace started to come over Turman and just as he was about to drift off to sleep the sound of clanking keys in the lock startled him back to reality. The news agencies were granted a zero-hour interview with the boys. They were handcuffed together and escorted to the main office of the Clark County jail where news reporters were waiting with paper and pencils in hand.

"Are you still maintaining you're innocent?" asked a reporter.

"Yes," replied Turman and Utah simultaneously.

"What if you're found guilty?"

"I think we have a good jury," responded Turman to the reporter's question, "I'm sure they'll analyze the evidence and be fair in whatever they decide."

"What do you plan to do if you're acquitted?"

"I want to be able to leave Washington State. There's no way we can live here and get a fair shake with all that's happened," said Turman.

Shortly after the interview with the brothers, 12 people had just reached a verdict. The jury retired for deliberation at 4:00 on the afternoon of June 28, 1950. They took a dinner break at 6:00 in the evening and then returned to be locked back up in the jury room for an additional two hours. At 10:45 PM the foreman knocked on the door to signal that a verdict had been reached.

Both defense attorneys were easy to reach because they had remained at the courthouse all evening. In the courtroom the final stage was set. There was Judge Cushing at the helm, the defense team and the two brothers seated at the defense table. However, no representation was present at the prosecution's table. Utah's bride of seven months was seated in a bench right behind her husband. Beyond that there were approximately 50 other people in attendance to hear the late night verdict.

Jo Ann's mother was absent as the verdict was being handed down. She had left the courtroom for the last time the day before. In a beautiful moment of Christian charity, Mrs. Dewey had rested her hand on Eunice Wilson's shoulder and said softly with sympathy, "Have courage."

Eunice Wilson and her daughter Patricia were supporting each other and other family members in the hallway just outside the courtroom.

As the last juror climbed into the jury box and stood in front of seat number 12 for the last time, Judge Cushing asked, "Has the jury reached a verdict?"

"Yes we have your honor," said Robert Davies, the elected foreman.

"Hand the verdict to the bailiff," directed the judge.

The bailiff, Al Cox took the paper from the foreman and handed it to the judge. Cushing read it and handed it back to the bailiff who in turn gave it to Miss Wilma Schmidt the courtroom clerk.

"Both defendants will rise and face the jury as the clerk reads the verdict," said the judge as he addressed the accused.

Miss Schmidt read the verdicts to a hushed and tense courtroom, "We the jury in the case of State verses Wilson find the defendants Turman Gallile Wilson and Utah Eugene Wilson guilty of the kidnap and murder of Jo Ann Dewey."

A mixed reaction in the crowd broke out as the news reporters clambered over one another to try to be the first one to a phone. Lucille Wilson ran sobbing from the courtroom and bumped right into Eunice and Patricia who realized instantly from her reaction that the verdict was not a favorable one. Eunice took the news with the same stoicism as her two sons but the boy's sister, Patricia put her head on her mother's shoulder and wept.

Back inside the courtroom the disappointment at the outcome of the trial was evident in the faces of Goodman and Clement as they looked at each other in disbelief.

"I would like to commend each and every one of you jurors for your patience during the long hours of this trial. I would also like to praise each and every one of you for the courage you have shown to perform your duties as citizens of these United States of America. Thank you all, this jury is hereby dismissed," concluded the judge as he banged his gavel for the last time in the case.

Reporters questioned Goodman and Clement who were very disappointed at the short length of time of less than six hours it took the jury to hand down two death sentences.

The prosecuting attorney left before the verdict came in and couldn't be found for a final comment. It was discovered later that he had taken off for a vacation in Canada. After he returned from vacation he polled the jurors and summarized their collective thoughts into a short brief which he released to the public as follows:

"While they (the jury) were very negative in their attitude at the beginning of the case it was the evidence, the conduct, the expressions and the statements which they heard in court that positively convinced them of the guilt of the Wilson brothers."

On Thursday June 29th, 1950 the news headline read; WILSON'S MUST HANG.

CHAPTER FIFTEEN

"THE APPEALS"

The Wilson brothers stayed in the Clark County jail under the watchful eye of Sheriff Anderson until their sentencing hearing on August 9, 1950. At that time it was ordered that Turman and Utah Wilson; "be punished by the infliction of the death penalty by hanging by the neck until dead as provided by law."

The fight to save the youths from the hangman had begun as their personal status changed from infamy to notoriety and continued press coverage detailed their plight. This unique situation brought the whole Wilson clan closer together. A family that was once insignificant "Dust Bowl Migrants" were now the center of mass media attention.

On the morning of Thursday, May 10, 1951 all nine judges of the Washington Supreme Court decided that the Wilson brothers had received a fair trial. The appeal submitted by the defense attorneys specifically stressed the boy's denial of their right of explanation for flight. Goodman pleaded that a defendant should have the right to explain the reason for his fear and his flight. During the trial Judge Cushing sustained every objection by Jones regarding Utah being accused of stealing a power saw. Therefore the jury was denied Utah's explanation of his state of mind which prompted his flight and subsequent suspicious conduct.

Following the Supreme Court's decision Goodman and Clement issued the following statement to the newspapers:

> *"We are shocked over the decision of the Washington Supreme Court. We believe the kidnap and murder charges against Turman and Utah Wilson would never have been made had it not been for Turman's record and the attitude of certain Vancouver police officers towards him since his release from prison. Indeed the state's entire case was based solely on circumstantial evidence and mere suspicion. We believe the boys are absolutely innocent and will reserve further commitment until we have had the opportunity to read the court's decision."*

The prosecuting attorney responded with a statement of his own as follows:

> *"I was of course very pleased to have the court's opinion upholding the jury decision for it had been a very strenuous case and the lower court had really been most conscientious in affording a fair*

> *trial and our office had been most*
> *concerned to see that this was*
> *accomplished and that justice was*
> *done."*

Judge Cushing expressed extreme gratification upon hearing the court's decision by making his own following statement on behalf of the judicial system:

> *"the object of the court is to see that*
> *everyone gets a fair trial and it is of*
> *prime importance that all judges make*
> *sure people respect the court system."*

On the day the Supreme Court's decision was handed down Turman and Utah had spent almost a full year in the Clark County jail in Vancouver, Washington. Upon receiving the news they were led in handcuffs to the jail's office where six news reporters were waiting to take statements from them.

Turman did most of the talking during the questioning. Both boys admitted that the Supreme Court's decision was a blow to their hope. They also stated that the police, especially Detectives Borgan and Ulmer had tried for a long time to pin felonies on them and now it looked like they had succeeded.

After their interview, preparations were made and the boys were sent to the State Penitentiary in Walla Walla, Washington. During Utah's first summer at Walla Walla him and Lucille got divorced. Even though she believed in her husband's innocence she couldn't take the separation and continued spotlight from the media. Six months into their stay at the penitentiary Utah received a letter from the ex-sheriff, Earl Anderson. He took the first pictures of Jo Ann's mutilated body that was snagged on the sand bar in the Wind River, a very remote place in Skamania County. He was present at the autopsy and he was one of the officers to bring the boys back from Sacramento. He was also subpoenaed to testify at the trial but the prosecutor never called him to the stand. Anderson worked very hard on the case but when he was asked by the Hazel Dell Grange to step down from his office because of all the bungling that went on during the investigation he tried to find some kind of closure on his own and wrote a letter to Utah.

The letter was dated Monday November 26, 1951, he wrote the following:

> *"Well young fellow, I guess you realize that some of us have 'guts' enough to stand up and get counted for what we know is right. The tinhorn politicians of Vancouver aided by The Columbian have been fooling the public in Clark County for a long time and they did a good job of fooling the public about the Jo Ann Dewey murder and about myself. Can you imagine clowns even got themselves elected to office because a young girl was murdered? It couldn't have happened anywhere but in Vancouver. Well, they didn't want me in office because I was too honest, too*

human and too much for the underdog. Well, they did me a favor, I am glad to be out of the rotten mess and believe me it is a rotten mess as I know it from the inside. No injustice ever prevailed for long. It is indeed unfortunate that you must pay the supreme penalty in order to focus public attention on the phony justice that prevails at the present time.

Remember what the preacher said? 'We pray to God those responsible for the death of Jo Ann Dewey be brought to justice.' Let me repeat when the state imposes the court's sentence upon you the preacher's prayers will <u>not</u> have been answered. You know this is true and I fully understand why you keep your mouth shut. Anything you say would be so badly distorted to fool the public that you wouldn't recognize it.

Utah, you know that I played the game with my cards face up and I have no regrets. I imagine that a lot of us would do things differently if we had our lives to live over and I am sure you would. I am sure you would say that I played the game square with you and I did everything possible for you consistent with my position as Sheriff. Now you can do something for me..."

The ex-sheriff ended his letter with nine cryptographic questions about Jo Ann's abduction and her death. Utah never replied.

Washington State law is such that a prisoner must be brought before the original judge to be given a new execution date. With every stay of execution there also came a new hanging date set by Judge Cushing. Like a thorn in his flesh he thought he'd never be rid of the Wilson brothers. On one of these sentencing trips Utah fell ill. Dr. Dennis Seacat was called to the County Jail where he dictated the following diagnosis:

> *"I am questioning the patient. He gave a history of having been last perfectly well until one month ago when he developed epi-gastric distress. He was seen at the prison hospital where a diagnosis of nervous gastritis was made and laxatives and aspirin were prescribed. This discomfort continued off and on until approximately three days ago when he developed, according to his story, pain in the lower quadrant. This pain has gradually become worse during the last two days and following the ride from Walla Walla he became nauseated and vomited, following which the pain in the right lower quadrant became intensified. On examination the temperature was ninety-nine, throat was clear, heart and lungs normal, abdomen*

*was soft with subjective tenderness and
slight rebound tenderness.*

> *In consideration of these findings
the following procedure was taken;
600,000 units of penicillin was given, a
blood and urine sample was taken which
follows the routine Armed Forces
conservative management of possible
appendicitis. We feel that with the
foregoing management that Utah Wilson
even though he may have acute
appendicitis can safely make the trip
back to Walla Walla. It is now 5:50 AM
and the scheduled leaving time is
approximately 9:30 AM."*

Following the diagnosis, Utah was loaded up in the
black paddy wagon and sent traveling across the entire
State of Washington with acute appendicitis –
miraculously he survived.

On February 11, 1952 the Wilson brothers had
been in the Washington State Penitentiary for 11
months. Warden John Cranor received a personal letter
from the boy's mother that day it read:

> *"Dear Mr. Cranor, upon my visit with
Turman and Utah they requested a
strong desire to have Reverend and Mrs.
Morgan as their spiritual advisors.
Since my visit I learned that Mrs.
Morgan was denied admittance to see
Turman and Utah. It is because of Mr.*

and Mrs. Morgan's wonderful understanding of the works of the Lord that Turman and Utah have taken their gracious stand with the Lord; being a Christian man yourself I know you can understand my sentiments. I would appreciate your kind consideration if you grant Turman and Utah's wish by allowing Mr. and Mrs. Morgan admittance anytime they wish to see the boys. Knowing you shall give this matter your kindest consideration I will remain sincerely yours, Mrs. Eunice Wilson, Mother of Turman and Utah Wilson."

The warden responded by officially designating Mr. Frank Morgan to be the spiritual advisor but his wife could not be included in that designation. Their spiritual advisor, Reverend Morgan also believed in their innocence. He sought and received an audience with the governor. He also inspired the Youth for Christ organization to jump into the Wilson brother's fight for life. The organization sent its national secretary to Walla Walla to direct a protest. The secretary rented a sound truck and slowly drove through the streets of Walla Walla broadcasting through a bullhorn mounted on top of the truck what was labeled "The True Story of The Wilson Brothers."

The extensive inquiries received from people throughout the Pacific Northwest clearly indicated the public's concern over the welfare of the boys. At that time Washington State's Governor was Arthur B. Langlie. He was hesitant to get involved with such a hot issue during an election year but on the other hand public pressure was forcing him to do something authoritative. This led him to request that Erle Stanley Gardner get involved.

Gardner had a decade of experience as a lawyer and was the well-known mystery writer who created Perry Mason. In the fifties Gardner was broadcast over the airways on a radio program called the "Court of Last Resort". Upon the governor's request he put together a staff of experts. One of the experts was Alex Gregory, a scientific interrogator and lie detector specialist who was also the president of the "Society for the Detection of Deception."

When Gardner was asked how good is the polygraph and how accurate Gregory's conclusions are? He responded; "This is something like the question, how good is a camera? Some people take beautiful photographs with a camera others take fuzzy pictures that are meaningless. Alex Gregory is one of the most competent polygraph men I know."

After Gregory administered the lie detector test it proved to be inconclusive. Gardner decided that; "because our group is composed of busy men who are donating as much of their time as is possible to aid the cause of justice, we feel other cases demanding our attention are more worthy of consideration. Our committee can only work in certain limited cases where a defendant who has been wrongfully convicted feels free to tell us everything he knows and where facts are currently available which when properly interpreted may throw new light on the subject such conditions do not exist in the present case."

After the lie detector's inconclusive results, Erle Stanley Gardner faded out of the picture that was the Wilson Brother's lives. Then life went routinely on in the penitentiary for the condemned pair. They were confined in separate cells on death row, but saw each other daily during calisthenics.

Rassi Wilson, the boy's older brother who was confined in the Oregon State Penitentiary in Salem requested permission to play chess by mail with his two brothers. The warden responded to the request by stating:

> *"I see no reason why we should make special concessions in the case of the Wilson brothers by permitting them to carry on a game of chess by mail. I am recommending that such action be not approved."*

Even if the warden would have allowed the game to take place it would have been a very long, drawn out game, since at that time inmates were permitted to write only one letter to a relative every other day.

During each of the four appeals and stays of executions between the years 1951 and 1952 Turman and Utah suffered agonizing conflict between the hope of the truth setting them free and the need to prepare for death.

A plea to the Governor for help composed in a letter written by the older of the two brothers stated the following:

"My name is Turman Wilson, myself and my brother Utah have been sentenced to be hanged on August 20, 1951. We were convicted in Clark County, Washington of kidnapping and murdering a young girl by the name of Jo Ann Dewey. We appealed to the Washington Supreme Court because we are innocent. The Supreme Court has upheld the conviction but included in the decision of the trial was that legal evidence was held from the jury.

Now sir, I'll not hesitate to say because it is the truth that the whole investigation into the Dewey case was not conducted from the stand point of actually apprehending the people that committed those crimes but only from the stand point of clearing the police books of the crime. The only member of the Dewey family that my brother Utah or myself have ever seen at all was Mrs. Dewey, Jo Ann's mother and that was in the court room during the trial.

After we were charged with those crimes we came into the courtroom believing that we would receive our lawful rights. All we could do was to present that evidence to the jury and then wait and hope. We tried to present that evidence but the most important part of our legal evidence was held from the jury. Because that evidence was the only meaning of our actions and our actions were the thing that gave the police the idea that they could put those crimes on our shoulders.

The same three police which were mainly connected with the Dewey case are the same ones who have constantly threatened to put me back into the Penitentiary. Their names as the record will show are Forsbeck, Borgan and Lord. Those three officers out of the hundred or more of Clark County are the only ones who had constantly tried to pin crimes on to me which I had never even heard of.

Now Sir, if my brother and I were guilty of those crimes we would be the last to contend otherwise. It just isn't right at all that we should have to suffer for those crimes while the people who have committed them are allowed to continue to be free. We have tried to tell the truth throughout this whole affair and that is the best we could do. There was a deputy sheriff in Vancouver by the name of Bill Scott who was convinced of our innocence and he was arranging to have a test conducted with the lie detectors for my brother and myself but the District Attorney Mr. Jones order him to lay off.

The one fact of this whole matter is that Jo Ann Dewey is dead. Therefore justice and society owe it to her to do all that is possible to apprehend the persons who have cheated her of life. So it just isn't right that we should pay for those crimes just for the purpose of relieving the police of the pressure that was being put on them by the public for their blundering. I would like to ask you to analyze the situation from start to the present time and if there is anything that you can possibly do to help us and justice it will be deeply appreciated and should you feel that you cannot do anything then I assure you that we will feel that the consideration that you give the matter will have been an honest consideration. Thank you, very sincerely, Turman G. Wilson.

Another stay of execution from the governor followed this letter. However like sand through an hourglass everything runs out in life and the fifth and final execution date with the hangman had come. Preparations were in order and the boys got what the penal system called a "clean up". It was their last shave. Lieutenant Norwood brought Turman and Utah from their separate cells to Wing One for the clean up ritual. The lieutenant took a seat in the barber's chair while Turman started shaving himself. Utah sat down on a bench against the wall. As Turman was shaving the Lieutenant got up from the barber's chair to go over and sit by Utah. After Turman had finished shaving, he washed his face and neck then dusted his smooth skin with talcum powder. He walked over to the bench as Utah got up to begin the final hygiene regiment of his life. He walked over to the corner washbowl and studied his face in the large oval mirror that hung above the basin for a moment then began lathering his face. When he had finished he wiped the remnants of lather from his face and neck. A crowd of inmates had gathered outside the large picture window to watch the boys shave, Utah smiled at them. Even in prison their last shave drew a crowd.

To prepare them for hanging, the boys were carefully weighed and measured in order to calculate the exact length of rope needed so as to sever the spinal cord without detaching the head. Even a minor miscalculation may cause only trauma to the spinal cord and the prisoner then becomes a victim of slow strangulation or decapitation. Their measurements were also taken for another reason. In 1953 those who were to be executed got a brand new suit.

As the final minutes of their lives ticked by, Turman wrote his last words addressed to the public; "Utah and I feel that we and our lawyers have done all within the reaches of righteousness to show our innocence. We have told the truth even though the jury wasn't allowed to hear it. We have no choice but to put our trust in God. We feel that if we do die for this crime that some day the facts will be uncovered to show our innocence."

Utah had his spiritual advisor write for him as he dictated the following; "Throughout this whole ordeal Turman and I have told the truth. There has been the inference given many times that in order to save my brother I offered him an alibi. This is definitely not true. Neither of us had a thing to do with neither the Jo Ann Dewey abduction nor her murder. We felt that when we went to court all we had to do was stick to the truth and we would get justice and be set free. We were convicted on planted evidence and suspicion. We thank all the kind people who believe in us. We are also thankful for a wonderful God who has been by our sides constantly."

After sealing their last words in an envelope the boys chose their favorite foods for their last meal. The menu consisted of roasted pheasant with dressing and gravy along with a salad, French fries, fresh brown bread and butter. For dessert they had banana cream pie, pineapple cream pie and ice cream. They had milk to drink with their meal and coffee with their dessert. Even though all these foods were their favorites it was hard to swallow their meal just as it was hard to swallow how they were framed and railroaded to the gallows.

It was 11:30 PM on Friday, January 2, 1953. The decision as to who would be hung first was given to the boys to decide. Together they decided Turman should ascend the gallows first. Just before they were to be accompanied to the gallows by Reverend Morgan the warden delivered a last minute telegram. It came from the Oregon State Penitentiary it was from their older brother Rassi. The telegram of encouragement read; "I love you with all my heart and I am praying for you. May God bless you until we meet again."

Half an hour later it was midnight January 3, 1953. The weather was lousy. A huge full moon lit up the snow covered ground, ice clung to the gallow steps. Despite the cold night and terrible weather conditions, policemen, reporters, inmates and witnesses in addition to a large assembly of public spectators gathered to watch the open spectacle.

Turman was wearing a perfectly tailored, brown suit. He shivered from the cold as he lifted a shaky right leg up and onto the first frozen wooden step. Upon reaching the top platform a black cloth was pulled over his head. Delicate snowflakes clung to the black hood seconds before melting as a carefully measured length of rope was placed around his neck and tightened. A nod was given and the lever pulled. The trapdoor under Turman's feet gave way and he dropped through the air. The executioner had done his job well and prisoner number 23441 was dead at 12:17 AM on January 3, 1953.

By having his brother go first Utah knew he could climb the gallow steps with dignity as well as his brother before him had. Wearing his new blue suit, white dress shirt and tie, he climbed up the stairs to put his neck in the noose. In like manner prisoner number 23442 was dead at 12:24 AM on January 3, 1953.

The two limp bodies were empty vessels without a soul. The vessels were handled by the living who had a job to do, the job of fingerprinting and some paperwork. A "Record Of Death" was filled out as the warden pressed Turman's lifeless right index finger onto a pad of black ink then rolled the impression onto the paper. Then he did the same thing to the younger boy.

The corpses were taken to the DeWitt Funeral Home in Walla Walla, Washington where they were made up for an open casket funeral. Later the bodies were driven back to Vancouver, Washington. Plans were made for the Wilson's funeral to be held at the Playhouse Theatre where the boys were watching "Captain" movies on the night Jo Ann was abducted. After two and a half years the old building on Morrison Street in Portland, Oregon had been abandoned as a theatre and was being used for religious meetings and public gatherings. However numerous protests arose objecting on the grounds that a public spectacle was being made of the services. The idea was quickly abandoned and the funeral was held at the Church of God in Fern Prairie, Washington.

Over one hundred people attended the funeral while Reverend Morgan presided, "they had smiles on their faces" recited the preacher to a packed church, "I know in my heart Turman and Utah gave their lives for a crime they didn't commit. I believe they are walking the golden streets of Heaven this very afternoon."

After the funeral services the two caskets were loaded into the back of the hearse and hauled to the Camas Cemetery. Their brother's Glen and Grant Wilson were among the twelve pallbearers who carried the caskets up the gravel walkway towards the far edge of the cemetery. Eunice Wilson clutched her son's Bibles to her bosom as she walked in the procession and wept.

Towards the end of the graveside services an old man who seemed to have appeared out of nowhere came walking from the back of the crowd and up the wet grassy hill towards the mourners. He declared he was having a vision. In this vision he proclaimed that he saw the faces of the killers of the Dewey girl and that they were not the faces of Turman or Utah Wilson.

CONCLUSION

It was the mid 1990's not the early fifties. But to the Propagator the memory that flooded her thoughts seemed like yesterday.

Sometimes an answer to a mystery can bring up more questions, however this time something was different. The Propagator was finally unburdened of an invisible backpack that she had been carrying around for over 40 years. Through the words of a song, she was freed from years of keeping the secret concerning Jo Ann Dewey's death. Gone was the oppression hanging over her mind and body of her father's constant threat, "If you tell, I'll do the same thing to you."

I believe the true injustice is in the fact that real predators continue to stalk neighborhoods in towns and cities across the country and throughout the world and no one gives a voice to the victims.

What happened over a half century ago was definitely unjust treatment, there's no doubt in the Propagator's mind that her father, would have followed through on his threats. Now the fear is gone from her soul, she can sing it to the world if she wants to, because her God will never leave her nor forsake her.

Faith stolen, families destroyed, marriages dissolved, innocent lives taken in a split second. Agony that will last forever, for the Dewey and Wilson families, the Propagator's family and for many other families as well.

The moon that shines in the sky today is the same moon that witnessed the Propagator's innocence stolen, a teenager sacrificed and mutilated, two brothers hung for a murder they didn't commit, second, third and fourth generations haunted by this incident, what could possibly come out of this?

God is no respecter of the time frame that we human beings live in. In fact our lives are but vapors in comparison to eternity and eternal things. There is no way to measure earthly events by heavenly standards. There may be no justice served here on earth but God is the final Judge and no yard stick or ticking clock can change the past, present or future.

Never forget that God is the Alpha, the Omega, the Beginning and the End.

Made in United States
Troutdale, OR
02/12/2025

28934324R00106